All I Know So Far

by: Nicole Zelniker

All I Know So Far

Inked in Gray Press

InkedinGray.com

ISBN Paperback: 978-1-952969-24-9

ISBN Ebook: 978-1-952969-25-6

Cover Design by Squidblot Arts

PRAISE FOR NICOLE ZELNIKER

"*All I Know So Far* paints a nuanced portrait of self-discovery, reconciliation, and the impact of family in all its complicated forms. A deeply touching read for anyone who's ever had to pick up the pieces when life falls apart."

— SYDNEY LANGFORD, AUTHOR OF *THE LOUDEST SILENCE*

"An intimately told coming-of-age story that is full of honesty and incredibly queer. *All I Know So Far* is the kind of book that will be a comfort to young people who need to be reminded that they are not alone, they are loved, and they are enough for this world."

— JONNY GARZA VILLA, AWARD-WINNING AUTHOR OF STONEWALL HONOR BOOK *ANDER & SANTI WERE HERE*

"Relatable and funny, *All I Know So Far* is densely packed with teen milestones, a story about the challenges of navigating familial, platonic, and romantic relationships when you don't quite know who you are yet."

— AARON H. ACEVES, AUTHOR OF *THIS IS WHY THEY HATE US*

"*All I Know So Far* is a gorgeous coming-of-age tale full of pain, recovery, and family. Queer joy is brimming over the edges of this novel. Zelniker writes Avery's story with deftness and humor, and by the end I was begging for another hundred pages. I didn't want to say goodbye to these characters."

— EMME LUND, AUTHOR OF *THE BOY WITH A BIRD IN HIS CHEST*

"*All I Know So Far* shows so many different sides to queerness and how we can support each other's differences. The relationship between Avery and their brother Lucas is sweet, tender, and very real. It anchors the story as these two characters grow and learn alongside each other. Avery's relatable voice and the epistolary style kept me from putting the book down and made it a quick and easy read."

— OLIVIA NEAL, AUTHOR OF *BLUE RIDGE CALLING*

"In a voice at once tender, raw, and completely true, Nicole Zelniker beautifully brings Avery Marsh – and all their joys, struggles, frustrations, and moments of becoming – to life. *All I Know So Far* is an intimate and transportive portrait of the ways friendship and found (and re-found) family can piece us back together when life scatters us apart."

— NATALIA SYLVESTER, AUTHOR OF SCHNEIDER FAMILY AWARD BELPRÉ AWARD HONOR BOOK, *BREATHE AND COUNT BACK FROM TEN*

"In *All I Know So Far*, Zelniker paints a stunning triptych. On the left, a colorful coming-of-age through a senior year in upheaval. In the middle, a swirling sunset of queerness, first love, and chronic pain. On the right, a vibrant portrait of what it means to be family. A museum-quality work brimming with heart."

— MARISSA ELLER, AUTHOR OF JOINED AT THE JOINTS

*To Allison, without
whom Avery's story
would not exist.*

TRIGGER WARNINGS

The following page lists several content warnings for *All I Know So Far*. If you don't like to read content warnings before you read a book, that's fine! Please skip this page and read on.

Otherwise, know that this book contains content that could be difficult for some readers, including depictions of ableism, characters struggling with their mental health, child neglect, chronic pain, death and grief, homophobia, medical trauma, and transphobia. There is also mention of a character's suicide attempt before the events of the book.

Please feel free to reach out at nicolezelniker.com/contact for any clarifying questions or concerns and remember to take care of your mental health.

You matter.

I can't actually remember the last time I saw my parents touch, but it was probably by accident. Maybe Mom passed Dad the remote from the opposite end of the couch and their fingers brushed or Dad squeezed by Mom on his way out of the kitchen. My parents haven't been in love since I was, like, ten, and I get that it must suck to sleep in the same bed as someone who gets more excited when the waiter at Olive Garden brings out the breadsticks than when you come home from a long day at the office, but they couldn't have waited until after I graduated high school to get a divorce? Seriously?

Maybe I should be glad there wasn't a big legal battle. My friend Vera's parents got divorced when we were in fourth grade and it was a freaking circus. They'd both show up to pick up, screaming at each other until security came and Vera and her sister had to go home with their aunt instead. For real, this happened at least three times. I am grateful my parents don't care enough to stage a whole production in the Trader Joe's parking lot, but it would be nice if either of them wanted me to even stay in the state. Instead, they're shipping me off to my older brother – who I haven't seen in person in three years – because apparently getting divorced means they don't have to be parents anymore either.

So now I'm writing this on my flight from hell, aka express from LAX to Middle-of-Nowhere, Virginia. The two men next to me haven't shut up once in the last four hours, the kid behind me won't stop screaming, and there's something sticky under my shoe I don't even want to identify. The good news is that no one has looked twice at the teenager in the window seat crying their eyes out at the thought of spending the next year with her absentee brother and his mysterious girlfriend in a state she's never even visited.

I'm amazed Lucas agreed to this at all. Most of the time he acts like I don't exist, which sucks because we were really close when I was a kid. He's eight years older than I am, so he used to invent all kinds of games to keep me entertained. Example: The Song Game, where one of us would hum a song and the other would try to guess what the song was. Even when he was a teenager, he always played with me if I asked. He's technically my half-brother, but I never really thought about any of that until the day he went off to college across the country and never looked back. He's been with his girlfriend, Jess, for a year and a half, and they've been living together for six months, but Mom and I have only met her once over FaceTime on a call that lasted approximately ten minutes.

The one silver lining in the drama that has become my life is Xio. Xio Soto was my best friend from kindergarten through third grade, until their mom got a job at the university in Mill-boro, the same one Lucas works at now. I messaged Xio when Mom told me I was moving, and it turns out we'll be at the same school. It's the most exciting thing about this whole fiasco, but to be fair, the bar is low.

We're about to land so I can transfer to a second, hopefully less sticky plane. Wishing myself good luck because clearly no one else will.

*I*t's been less than twenty-four hours and I don't know anything anymore.

Lucas picked me up at the airport on time because he's never been late for anything in his life. He found me outside arrivals and did that awkward side hug thing men do when they don't actually know how to greet people. It's strange to see him after so long because until we're face to face, it's easy to forget we're related. Like, very obviously related. We're both pretty tan for white people, with blue-black hair and the same freckles splashed across our noses. The biggest difference now is that I got bangs last month and Lucas's hair is wildly curly, but other than that, it's like looking at the older, guy version of me. We both look like Mom, except that Mom is in a weird blonde phase we don't talk about.

It's August, but my brother is apparently a masochist because he showed up to what's got to be the smallest airport in North America wearing dark washed jeans and a blazer. I'm sorry, but who are you trying to impress, sir? It's five o'clock on a Sunday and now I'm second guessing my choice to wear an oversized T-shirt and leggings on a multi-hour flight like a normal person.

We got in his Kia and stared at each other in an unspoken game of chicken. Lucas cracked by the time he pulled onto the highway. "How's Mom?" he asked.

"Fine." I shrugged. "Pretty good for someone about to end her second marriage." Lucas's dad died, to be fair, so it's not like this is going to be her second divorce, but it's still a second marriage.

Lucas clicked his blinker on and switched lanes. "That sounds right," he muttered. "How's your dad?"

"Fine." I haven't spoken to Dad in at least a week and I haven't seen him in almost three. He didn't come to say goodbye at the airport. "How's Jess?" I asked, even though I didn't really care. She seemed friendly enough when we spoke over the phone, but other than that and the fact that she was dating my brother, I knew nothing about her.

Lucas went quiet. Like, weirdly quiet. I almost thought I got his girlfriend's name wrong or something. He tapped a finger on the steering wheel and said, "There's something you should know before we get home." He took a breath. "Jess isn't really my girlfriend."

I frowned. "What? Why would you pretend to date someone?"

"I am dating someone," Lucas said. A little defensive, like he's not the one who just said he'd been lying to all of us for the last year and a half. Lucas met my eyes in the mirror, then looked away. "His name is Ezra."

Excuse me, was he joking? My perfect older brother, the one my mom constantly said I should be more like, was dating a man. The same brother who hadn't said jack when I came out as bi or changed my name to Avery and my pronouns to "she/they" on social media has a boyfriend named *Ezra*. Based solely on how Mom reacted to my own coming out (both times), I see why he wouldn't have told her growing up. She wasn't violent and she didn't threaten to disown me or anything, but she and Dad both did the whole "it's a phase" thing and pretended like it wasn't happening. It was unnerving how easily they could ignore what I very determinedly paraded in front of their faces. I got a Reneé Rapp poster for my room and everything. But now, Lucas lived across the country. He didn't even have to see them. And he had a queer sibling, for crying out loud!

Lucas's grip on the steering wheel tightened. "I'm sorry I didn't tell you," he went on when I didn't say anything. "Ezra said I should. I wasn't ready though, if it got back to Mom . . ."

"I wouldn't have outed you," I said loudly.

Lucas might have flinched a little. "I know," he said. We didn't speak for the rest of the ride, minus when Lucas asked me what I wanted from takeout.

Driving through Millboro depressed me. It's a fine town, I guess, but it's still a town. Instead of sky-scraping buildings, tiny brick dwellings lined the sidewalk. Instead of towering palm trees, spindly, anonymous, near-bushes stuck up from the ground every block or so. A deli and a book store surrounded the Chinese place we got our food from. Both were closed and it wasn't even nine o'clock. In fact, I don't think anything was open but the Chinese place.

We pulled up in front of the house with a bag of takeout, which smelled more like the kind of stir fry Mom would make at home than actual Chinese food, and my luggage. I do have to admit, the house is pretty cute. It's one story and pale blue with dark accents and a small garden by the entrance.

Lucas unlocked the door and I followed him inside. The entryway is right next to the living room, so I immediately saw the boyfriend on the couch. He wore a tank top that showed off the tattoo on his left bicep, birds taking flight from his elbow to his shoulder. I didn't see any other tattoos, but he also wore a silver wrist brace, so there could have been something under that. He had five o'clock shadow, like Chris Hemsworth in *The Avengers*-style, but dark brown instead of blonde.

Ezra stood and smiled at me. "It's great to meet you, Avery."

"Yeah. You, too." Surreal to meet someone you thought was a five-foot Asian woman who turned out to be a six-foot Latino man, but sure, let's go with 'great.'

He quirked an eyebrow. "Expecting Jess?"

"Kind of," I admitted. Lucas grimaced, as if this wasn't his fault in the first place. Jeez.

He shuffled his feet and held out the yellow plastic bag for Ezra's inspection. "We stopped for takeout on the way," he said. "I got your favorite."

"Excellent," Ezra quipped. "I'm starving." My brother isn't short, but Ezra still had a few inches on him. He leaned forward to kiss Lucas, which definitely didn't help the whole I'm-in-the-Twilight-Zone vibe of this whole day. Neither did the painfully soft look on Lucas's face when Ezra kissed him.

Mostly, conversation over dinner consisted of Ezra asking me questions about myself while Lucas picked at his lo mien. He asked me if I'd ever been to Virginia before (nope), if I'd started looking at colleges yet (sort of), and if I was sick of people asking me that yet (absolutely). He told me a little about himself, too. I asked about his tattoo and he told me he also has a semi-colon on the covered wrist and the outline of a New York skyline around his leg. He's from Chicago and moved to New

York when he was a teenager, which explains the skyline, and does communications for the local rape crisis center, which is so cool compared to doing college fundraising like Lucas does at Millboro. He's pansexual and demiromantic and he's been all over the U.S., but somehow found himself settling here with my socially awkward dork of a brother. The wrist brace isn't from a bar fight (my guess, mostly just to piss off Lucas), but from an arthritis flare because, in Ezra's words, "I'm actually about a hundred."

I shrugged. "I can't eat diary," I said. IBS thing. Not the same, but that's what I got. It's also chronic, but not constant, at least not for me. It's the kind of thing that's different for everyone.

Ezra laughed. "Neither can Lucas," he said.

I glanced at my brother. I hadn't known that, but I felt weird saying it. Like I was giving something up, but I didn't know what. Lucas continued to pick at his food. Ezra looked between us and hastily changed the subject.

After dinner, Lucas showed me to the guest room. My room now, he said. The only way I can describe it is very, very white. White walls, white drawers, white bookshelf, white sheets. Lucas looked around and said, "Most of your stuff should get here soon, so we'll be able to decorate however you'd like."

"Sure." As if this place would ever feel like mine.

Lucas left me to unpack with an invite to join him and Ezra in the living room whenever I'm done. I didn't bring a lot with me besides some clothes, my computer, and my phone and laptop chargers, since most of my stuff I could just ship. I finished unpacking about an hour ago. Mostly, I've been writing this, but I also did a quick search of Lucas's social media accounts. He only has Facebook and he never posts anything, which must be how he got away with being closeted for so long. If he has an Instagram or a Bluesky or anything, I can't find it. I added Ezra on Instagram and he approved my follow, but the only pic he has of Lucas is a group shot from a few months ago.

I also texted Xio and Mom to let them know I made it. Xio sent back three dancing women emojis, WELCOME in all caps, and a red heart. Mom hasn't responded.

An email from Mom to Lucas

From: carriemarsh99@gmail.com
To: lucaswilde@millboro.edu
Subject: Update

DEAR LUCAS,

Glad to hear everyone is settling in nicely! I appreciate you taking your sister in on such short notice. The divorce has been such a strain and it's wonderful to know I can count on you and Jess, even across the country. I'd love to talk to both of you soon, or even have you for a visit! Both of you are always welcome here, perhaps for Hanukkah? Let me know what you think.

I don't know if you know this, but your sister is going by "Avery" these days and calling herself a "they," whatever that means. Everyone her age seems to be doing the pronoun thing. She gets upset when you call her by her real name, so maybe you can avoid a few of the screaming matches she seems so prone to since she reached her teenage years. Barring a few incidents, I seem to remember you being much easier!

I shipped the rest of the boxes a few days ago, so they should get to you shortly. Say hello to your sister and Jess for me.

Much love,
Mom

When I was five, I started kindergarten, and I was a mess about it. I didn't know anyone in my class, since I'd gone to preschool the next town over, and I was super scared that none of the other kids would like me because they already had friends. I ended up missing the first day because I couldn't stop crying and Mom had to take me home.

Now multiply that by about a hundred. That's how I felt the first day of senior year, in a tiny town where everyone's known everyone else for years already. Thank God for Xio, who texted me last night and asked me if I wanted to meet up by the entrance ten minutes early. They saw me before I saw them and caught my arm. "I can't believe you're here," they cried.

"Oh my God!" I hugged them quickly and took a step back.

I've seen them on social media for years, of course, but it was totally strange to see them in person again. They looked more or less the same, but older, with longer hair, tips dyed slightly lighter than the roots, and half a dozen piercings along each ear. Xio used to live down the street from me with their parents and their little brother. From social media, I know they also have a sister and two cats, both tabbies, but I've never met them.

Xio gestured to their friends. "Avery, this is Zehra and Owen." Zehra was gorgeous with super curly hair down to her lower back and dark brown skin. She wore a white sundress with sunflowers on it from Torrid, a plus-size store I knew from shopping with Vera our mall back home. Owen was slightly shorter, with bright, dark eyes and a wine-colored birthmark just above his collar bone. I grinned at his shirt, which proclaimed him GAYSIAN AND PROUD. I never had queer friends in California, minus Xio, who didn't come out until after they moved.

"It's great to meet you," Zehra said with a wave. "We've heard so much about you."

Oh jeez. I know she meant that in a good way, but of course my anxiety-addled brain jumped immediately to all the embarrassing stories Xio could tell about eight-year-old me. "It's great to meet you too," I said.

The bell rang, a piercing screech that gave me chills even in the Virginia summer heat, and Zehra said, "Oh damn, I have to get to art. It's on the other side of the school."

"That's my first period too," I said.

Zehra lit up. "Really? I'll take you there." We went into the building together – red brick, like everything is in this town apparently – and started down the hall. Zehra told me a little bit about her and Owen. Zehra is autistic and hates crowds, which is why she tries to make it to first period before the hallways flood with too many bodies. I told her I felt similarly with my anxiety and she seemed to appreciate that. She's lived in Millboro pretty much her whole life and she's the last of her sisters to graduate. "So the teachers are always calling me by the wrong name," she said.

Owen moved here from North Carolina sophomore year, so at least there's one person I know who didn't grow up here. He's the president of the Pride club and will one hundred percent try to recruit me, Zehra said. In art, she introduced me to Ms. Chang, who's also the Pride advisor. "Welcome," Ms. Chang said. "Did you do art at your old school?"

I told her yes. Art is my favorite subject, especially painting and *especially* acrylics. There's something so satisfying about bringing something beautiful to life out of a blank page. I've thought about going to school for it next year, but Mom and Dad aren't fans of the idea. "You're throwing away your future," they like to say, even though I'm not particularly good at anything else. But now that I'm not living with them, maybe I can try it.

Besides Owen trying to recruit me at lunch (Zehra was right), Xio and the others mostly filled me in on everything I needed to know: Don't look Mr. Banks in the eye if you don't want to get called on in math; the art wing is weirdly annoying to get to, since the rest of the school is a circle and the art classes are on their own hallway. Things like that. After lunch, Owen and I had Spanish together and then after English with Xio, I finished the day with Mr. Will-Call-On-You-If-You're-Not-Careful Banks.

I didn't recognize anyone from my earlier classes, so I just sat in a random empty chair by the door toward the front of the room. The guy next to me did a double take and said, "Are you new? I don't think I know you."

"Yeah. I'm Avery."

"Devin," he said. He held out a hand and I shook it. He was cute, with sandy hair, big brown eyes, and a crooked but probably purposefully constructed smile. "Where are you from, Avery?"

"Los Angeles," I said. "I got here, like, a week ago."

"Oh damn, so you're new, new. Well, if you're not doing anything after school, I'd love to show you around."

I'd told Lucas I'd come right home after school, but he wouldn't be home until after five anyway. Ezra worked until half past four most days. I'd have plenty of time. Plus, no cute guys in lettermen jackets ever noticed me at my old school.

"Okay."

I barely paid attention to Mr. Banks for the rest of math. Lucky, I didn't get called on.

After school, Devin took me downtown and showed me all the fun spots. It was a little too cutesy for my taste, but I liked hearing about it from Devin's point of view. "Me and my friends sometimes come here for lunch," he said as we passed the deli. "And over there, they have some cool parties." He pointed to the huge building across the street.

"Is that what people do for fun around here?" I asked.

"Yeah. There are festivals sometimes, but I don't know. They're pretty boring. And the state fair happens once a year."

"We had stuff like that in L.A., but I never went."

"Really?" Devin asked. "What's it like in the big city?"

I shrugged. "Loud," I said. "Bright. It can be a lot, but I love it. There's always something to do."

"Well, maybe you'll have to show me some time," Devin said with a grin. I actually blushed and giggled like a little kid. I don't remember ever giggling like that before.

Devin took me home before five and I got started on my homework in the living room just as Ezra walked in. Lucas came home not much later. Lucas shrugged off his suit jacket and sat across from me. "How was your first day?" he asked.

"Good," I said. "Pretty good." Actually, anxiety-aside, it was great.

My stuff finally came! Lucas helped me unpack and now it finally feels like I can live in this too-white guest room. I have the nonbinary and bi flag watercolor prints on the walls I got from Etsy and the Reneé Rapp poster on the back of the door. I put a few selfies of my friends and I before I left California on a square cork board. My sheets came too and they're purple, so I can finally sleep in something that doesn't look like a snowstorm. I texted Mom to tell her my things are here, but as per usual, I don't expect her to reply for another three days. I haven't spoken to Dad at all. I wonder if he misses me.

School is pretty good so far. My favorite class is definitely art, but I knew that would happen, since it's always been my favorite subject. It's not just the art part of it, though. It's a lot of fun just hanging out with Zehra, and Ms. Chang is pretty cool.

"I like it, too," Zehra said when I told her. It's a very hands-on class because, duh, it's art, so Zehra and I mostly just talk while we paint or draw. "It's a lot easier for me to focus when I'm doing something physical," she said. "Someone always stares if I stim in other classes."

"People are assholes," I said. Zehra laughed. It turns out she's somehow both an art and science person, so she's just incredibly smart. She's taking AP everything and somehow has time to tutor freshmen and sophomores in bio.

Wednesdays, I do Pride after school (yes, Owen was successful in his recruitment), and it's fun to end the day with Ms. Chang, too, since she's my favorite teacher. She tries to hide it, but I think we're her favorite students. Xio is the Pride secretary and Zehra is treasurer, mostly because Owen begged them both. We'll all spend the first few months of the school year planning for the trip to DC, which happens in November.

When that's over we'll focus on the Gayla, which is a Valentine's dance Pride puts on every year. At least, that's what Owen said, but Xio and Zehra assured me it's also a lot of hanging out and playing board games and eating snacks. The last week of every month we watch movies – Zehra is already campaigning for *But I'm A Cheerleader* – but the last week of August was our first meeting of the school year, so that starts this month. We had a Pride at my school in L.A., but no one actually went to the meetings. A lot of my mostly straight friends thought our school was too progressive to need a Pride. Looking back, that's some pretty garbage irony.

Math is also one of my favorite classes, but only because I get to see Devin. We hang out maybe once a week after school now and we exchanged numbers and I know he's so close to asking me out and that's exciting, but also a little terrifying. I've never been in a real relationship before and I've only ever kissed

Andy Yu last year at homecoming. It was super awkward and I kept thinking about how his lips were chapped and his breath was hot in my mouth. We stopped pretty quickly. He was nice about it though, and we both decided we'd be better as friends.

Things are fine at home too. Besides my newly renovated room, Lucas keeps trying to get me to join him and Ezra for one of their Friday movie nights, which I keep dodging. Lucas's taste in movies is apparently old classics and anything Oscar bait. Not my style. I'm much more a fan of horror, Marvel movies, thrillers, things like that, though I love a good musical.

Ezra's been pretty cool and he's fluent in Spanish, so if I can grab him before Lucas gets home he'll sometimes 'help' me with my homework. Read: he does most of it, but he does actually help me study for tests. The three of us pretty much always eat dinner together at the dining room table, which is new for me. Mom and Dad used to eat in front of the TV all the time and it was lonely sometimes, but at the table I have to listen to Lucas and Ezra argue like every night. Not in an aggressive way, but it seems like they disagree about everything. Like last night it was about accessibility on Lucas's campus. "Some of the buildings are a hundred years old," Lucas was saying. "It's unrealistic to expect the school to replace them all with ADA certified buildings right away. Where would they hold classes?"

"Do it all over the summer." Ezra knows the campus well because he went to grad school at Millboro for communications. Again, so much cooler than finance.

"Summer classes."

"They could do half the buildings then."

"With what money?"

"The school has the money," Ezra said, "and even if they didn't, they could fundraise."

"It's a lot of money." Lucas turned to me and said, "Every time a student has a mobility-related disability on file, the school puts their classes on the ground floors." As if I wanted to take part in their repetitive non-arguing arguing.

"What about an athlete who gets an injury mid-semester?" Ezra asked. "Or what if there isn't a disability on file? I never told the school I had arthritis or fibro and I had loads of classes on the second floor of the communications building. The elevator was always breaking."

Fibro is fibromyalgia, I learned, which according to Google means you're tired and in pain a lot. It sounds awful and explains why Ezra goes to bed super early every night, though he pretty much never complains.

Lucas turned to face me. "What do you think, Avery?"

"Ezra's right," I said automatically.

"Why do you think so?"

I shrugged. "I mean it's crap that the school isn't accessible to everyone."

"The onus shouldn't be on the person with a disability to ask for accommodations every time," Ezra said, which is basically a fancier way of saying, "It's crap." He looked smug after I spoke up in agreement, much to Lucas's annoyance. I stifled a smile.

Lucas turned to me again. "How was school today, Avery?"

"Fine," I said. I finished my green beans and stood. "I'm going to finish my homework." Start, technically, but Lucas didn't need to know that my TikTok feed was more interesting than my AP lit homework.

"Okay," Lucas said. He seemed upset, but I don't know what he wants from me. I'm doing my best, but that never seems to be good enough for him.

I didn't expect to feel as close to my new friends as I do after a little under a month, but it feels like I've known them my whole life. Even with Xio, it's kind of like we never spent time apart. We're back to finishing each other's sentences and knowing what each other is thinking before we say it. I still miss my California friends, but at least I'm not alone.

A few weeks ago, we did a whole thing for Owen's birthday. Zehra distracted him with a lunch date downtown until it was time for the party, so Lucas dropped me off at Owen's house. Xio was on the porch with Owen's younger brother, Dylan, who's the year below us, and Owen's boyfriend, Connor, who lives the next town over. Dylan is Pakistani – he and Owen are both adopted – and nearly six feet tall, almost Ezra's height. Connor is white with shaggy, strawberry blonde hair and round, purple-rimmed glasses.

Xio introduced us and peered around me as Lucas drove away. "Damn, that's your brother?" they said when I approached. "He got pretty."

I pretended to gag. "That's so gross, oh my God. Aren't you ace?"

"I didn't say I wanted to sleep with him. Just, aesthetically, he's pretty." Connor laughed. I groaned and sat next to them on the porch. It's cool to have all queer friends, too. I had a lot of support from my friends in California, but it's different when the people you love just get it. Being the only one did feel isolating sometimes, especially when Mom and Dad refused to talk to me about it. I would sometimes look at Xio's Instagram and wonder what coming out was like for them, but I haven't told them that because it feels stalker-y.

Owen's mom came onto the porch and invited us all in for cider and asked if she could help us get ready. I met Owen's parents before, once, when they picked up me and Owen from Pride when his car was getting fixed and the school busses were long gone. Owen is the only one of us with a car. It's a super old convertible we're like ninety-eight percent sure won't make it through the end of the year. Zehra sometimes drives her mom's car, but both her parents work, so she can't bring it to school or anything. Besides, she lives close enough that she can walk there.

Anyway, Owen's parents are super nice. All my friends' parents are. I wouldn't say I'm jealous, but it is a little strange to see kids my age getting so much support. Owen talks openly about being gay and trans and his parents will ask questions about Pride and show their outrage at the homophobic kid in the hall who called Xio a slur the week before. Zehra's parents, too, are super supportive of her being bi, and even though

Xio's parents don't really understand they/them pronouns, they work really hard to use them and correct themselves when they mess up. I'm scared they think about my mom and dad sometimes and go, "Thank God my parents aren't like that."

Because Owen's parents were home, it wasn't a real party, but we invited the kids from Pride and we did manage to surprise Owen when he walked in with Zehra. His jaw dropped like in movies. He hugged me and Xio and kissed Connor on the cheek and we spent a lot of the night listening to Broadway soundtracks (yes, we're *those* gays) and playing games. I don't know. It was cool to make him so happy. His parents got him a new Adidas jacket because he's a slut for anything Adidas. He won't be caught dead in any other shoe. Apparently my Vans "pain" him, but Zehra's knock-off flats are worse. God forbid one of us wears Nike.

I've been hanging out more with Zehra too. We hung out for the first time one-on-one after school recently and walked to her place. Her parents were both at work, so we spread out or homework in the living room and pretended like we had any intention of doing it. "What do they do?" I asked about her parents.

"My mom's a lawyer," she said. "My dad teaches math at the middle school." She looked up at me without meeting my eyes. Zehra never makes eye contact, which I was surprised to realize is actually great for my anxiety and ADHD. It's so much easier to have a conversation with someone when you don't have to look at them. Zehra laughed when I told her this and said she thinks life would be better if we listened more to neurodivergent people.

"You live with your brother," she asked, "right?"

"Yeah, he works at the university," I said.

"Is he a professor?"

"No, he's in the finance department," I said. "It's totally

boring." Even teaching finance would be more exciting than actually doing it.

"It's not boring." I shot her a look and she laughed. "It's a little boring," she admitted. "How much older is he?"

"Eight years," I said. "He's technically my half-brother, but we grew up together until he left for college." Until he left me. My dad has two kids from his first marriage, too, but I don't think of them as my siblings as much as his other kids. Both of them live in L.A., but I almost never saw them growing up. After Dad divorced his first wife, the kids stayed with her, and they rarely spoke to him at all. "It's me and him and his boyfriend," I said. "That's actually how he came out to me. Like, 'Hey you know how I've been telling you I'm dating a woman? I lied. Meet my live-in boyfriend who you now also live with.'"

Zehra burst out laughing. "Wow, that's so much better than my coming out. I just told my parents I was bi and they were like, 'We knew that already, Zehra.'"

I grinned to myself. "Ideal. My parents thought I was joking and then asked me not to tell the rest of my family."

"Damn. No wonder your brother hasn't come out to them."

I shrugged. It sucked, but Lucas is an adult now. He should be able to say something, especially since he lives on the other side of the country. "Are you totally freaking out about submitting college apps?"

Zehra let me change the subject with no complaint and we spent the next however long griping about the common app and how scary it was to ask teachers for recommendations. I felt weird about writing to my old teachers and when I asked Ezra about it, he assured me a lot of the seniors would ask teachers they only had this year, too. I asked Ms. Chang, who's also writing recs for Xio and Zehra and Owen, and my Spanish teacher, who thinks I'm brilliant and doesn't know it's because Ezra helps me study. The last person I asked was my AP lit teacher, who gave me a look like, "You really have no one else to ask?" before agreeing out of pity.

Devin probably asked Mr. Banks, not that I would know. He's perfectly friendly when we sit together in math, but we haven't been hanging out as much. That's fine, but I liked him and I thought maybe he liked me too. It's ridiculous because we just met, but I can't help thinking we'd be so perfect together.

I finally got over my anxiety yesterday and asked Ms. Chang if she'd help me figure out which pieces to submit to schools. I also told her I was applying to only art schools, which is super scary to tell her as my art teacher because what if she thought I sucked? Then I'd have to sit in art class with her for the rest of the year and make awkward eye contact every once in a while.

We decided on some old watercolor and charcoal pieces, but we also just did an acrylic unit and that's my favorite thing to work in, so we picked the two I did for class. The first one was a portrait of Xio driving Owen's convertible. I didn't have a picture of that, so I had to paint it mostly from other photos and memory, but I think it came out pretty ok. The second was a still life of a bunch of makeup palettes and brushes from when Owen was doing Zehra's makeup one day after school. Turns out Ms. Chang doesn't think my art sucks, so that's exciting! At least, she says she doesn't.

After school, I took the bus home, since Xio's grounded for getting a B on a test, Zehra has family visiting all weekend, and Owen already has rehearsals for the fall band concert. Unfortunately, this meant I'd also run out of excuses, so when Lucas asked me for the eighty-five millionth time if I'd join him and Ezra for one of their boring movie nights, it was that or doom scroll through Instagram all night and look at how much fun my California friends were having without me while I couldn't even hang out with my Virginia friends.

Lucas dragged me out of the guest room at exactly eight o'clock because that man believes if he isn't exactly on time to something the world will explode, even if that something is a movie night in his own living room. He sat practically on top of Ezra on the couch, which, gross, so I sat on the armchair even though there was plenty of room. Ezra stopped scrolling through Netflix and asked me, "Do you like horror, Avery?"

I told him I love horror, and Lucas groaned. "Please don't make me," he said.

"What are some of your favorites?" Ezra asked.

"*Get Out*," I said immediately because Jordan Peele is a genius. "*Nope. Midsommar.*"

"Not *Us?*"

Lucas groaned louder. I ignored him. "It isn't streaming anywhere I can get it." Neither was *Get Out*, but my friend Haley back in L.A. borrowed her older brother's copy this summer before I left and we watched it with a bunch of our friends. That was the last time I saw most of them in person.

"I own it," Ezra said.

Lucas sighed and turned his face up to Ezra's. "You owe me."

Ezra laughed and kissed Lucas on the forehead. "I'll make it up to you."

Lucas grumbled something about popcorn and left while Ezra pulled up the movie. "I've been trying to get him to watch this with me for months," he said with a wink.

The popcorn bowl ended up being about fifty percent an actual popcorn bowl, fifty percent Lucas's shield from the TV. I might have also been a little scared at some points, but I said I wasn't just to bug Lucas. He glued himself to Ezra's side and buried his face in Ezra's shoulder on and off for the whole second half of the movie. Ezra kept his arm around Lucas and told him when he could look again. It was actually pretty cute, but I'd never tell them that. After the movie, Lucas glared at both of us. "I'm picking the next one," he said. He still had his arms around Ezra's waist in a death grip.

"Of course you will," Ezra said. He brought Lucas's head onto his shoulder, made eye contact with me, and shook his head once. I grinned.

"I'm going to have such nightmares," Lucas groaned.

"And I'll be right here when you do," Ezra promised. He kissed the tip of Lucas's nose.

"That's my cue to leave," I said. I untangled my legs from two of the obscene number of blankets on they kept in the living room and stood.

Lucas frowned. "You don't have to go."

I shrugged. Even if they weren't getting totally mushy, I'd had enough family bonding for one night.

"Ok," Lucas said. "Well. Do you mind taking the popcorn bowl with you?" I rolled my eyes, but I did take it, and Lucas beamed. The most ridiculous things make him happy.

Xio is still grounded tonight, but Owen doesn't have rehearsal and Zehra can get away from her cousins for a few hours, so I have an excuse not to spend the night with my older brother. It will be my first time hanging out with the two of them without Xio, but I'm ok with that. I really like them and I think they like me, too.

Last night wasn't that bad, though, for a family-bonding-movie-night. I might not hate doing another one, so long as Ezra keeps picking the movies.

*E*zra was the one to suggest apple picking in the first place. I wasn't sure I wanted to go, in part because Xio and Zehra are going to the state fair this weekend and in part because I've never actually been apple picking, but it seems like something happy couples bring their kids to instead of something teenagers do with their older brother and his boyfriend. Lucas promised we'd be home with plenty of time for the fair and Ezra said he and Lucas went last year and they saw plenty of people my age, so I got up at half past nine, threw on a checkered flannel, and met Lucas and Ezra in the kitchen. Lucas was at the freezer and Ezra had his leg stretched out on a second chair and a very Lucas-like grimace on his face. He turned to me and said, "Mind if I take a rain check on apples?"

Honestly, kind of. The whole thing was his idea and it wouldn't be nearly as fun without him. "Is everything ok?"

The grimace turned into an apologetic smile. "Arthritis flare," he said. "I'll be fine. I just can't walk."

That didn't seem "fine" to me, but I supposed Ezra knew best. Lucas handed him an ice pack from the freezer and Ezra pressed it against his knee over his sweatpants. "We're not just going to leave you here," Lucas said. Which was probably fair, but part of me was miffed that Lucas wanted to be alone with me just as much as I wanted to be alone with him, so not at all.

Ezra waved a hand. "I'm not dying. I'll just use my weed cream and sleep it off."

Lucas sighed. "It's not weed."

"CBD, whatever."

"What if it gets worse and you need something?"

"I'll use my cane." To me, Ezra said, "You still want to go, right?"

Not really, but I also wanted to make Lucas feel bad about him not wanting to spend any alone time with his sibling. "I'm game," I said.

Lucas looked at me, then back at Ezra. "You'll call if you need anything?" Amazing it was that easy, especially when he had the chance to argue with Ezra, his favorite thing in the world.

"Yes, yes," Ezra said. "Now go have a good time." A nice thought, but unlikely.

So, an hour later, Lucas and I started off through the apple orchard, each of us holding a dark green bag with the orchard's logo stamped on either side, awkwardly meeting each other's eyes and looking away again. That's when I realized I hadn't actually been alone with Lucas since he picked me up at the airport. Ezra always gets home before him and they're both up when I leave for school in the morning.

People gathered at the entryway, which is where vendors

sold cider and tourists took photos in front of the massive sign, so we started walking down the rows to a quiet-looking patch across the field. We got to the end of the row and I fiddled with a loose thread on my sleeve. "So, how did you and Ezra actually meet?" He'd supposedly met Jess through work, and the real Jess is a work friend, but that wasn't how he met Ezra.

Lucas's lips twitched. "We really did meet at the university, but we weren't colleagues. I'd started my job not too long before, but they stuck me on a panel last minute to talk about college finances because my supervisor had a family emergency." He plucked an apple from the tree and examined it. "Ezra was in the communications program at the time. He stood up during the Q&A portion and asked why there wasn't more funding allocated to the Queer Student Union's festival the next month when all the admin had just gotten big bonuses." He must have deemed the apple satisfactory because he put it in his bag.

"I didn't even know there was a festival happening," he continued. "It's annual, but like I said, I'd just started. Apparently, there'd been a big protest the year before because the university didn't give them anything and one of the admins had actually been funding a homophobic organization. Basically, Ezra called us out and I had no idea how to respond. I went to the festival the next month with Jess, actually, and I saw him there, so I thanked him for calling my attention to it."

I burst out laughing. "Sorry, the guy yells at you in front of the entire panel and you thanked him?" We rounded the corner and found a small cluster of trees with low-hanging, ruby red apples and no people in sight. I picked an apple from the tree, briefly examined it for bruises or holes, and put it in my bag when I couldn't find any.

"He was right," Lucas said with a shrug. "I like that he challenges me, you know? Anyway, after that we talked a while. He said something about my job being problematic, I said something about how he'd never get anything from the university if he kept insulting the finance department, and then we, um, we got together."

He picked another apple and stared at it a little too intensely. I wondered briefly why he was being so weird about it, until it clicked and my eyes widened in sheer horror. "Oh my God, Lucas, did you have sex at the festival?" I didn't really want to know, but I also had to. It's like when you drive by a car wreck and can't look away.

Lucas went redder than the apples. "No. The festival was outside." Each word came out quieter than the last.

I continued to speak at a normal volume. "So, you went inside." I can never step foot in Lucas' office.

"I'm not entirely sure this is an appropriate conversation to have with my little sibling."

I rolled my eyes and picked another apple. "So you fought, you had hate sex, then you went on a real date."

"More or less," Lucas muttered.

We started down the path again. "How come you haven't told Mom?" I asked. This time, I did lower my voice.

"My relationship with Mom is complicated," he said, sighing. Which is all well and good, but he still could have told me. Plus if he'd come out when I did, even just to me . . . I don't know. It would have made the whole thing less lonely.

"Does Ezra get flares a lot?" I asked.

"Sometimes. Stress always makes it worse, especially with the fibro. His doctors are trying to get insurance to approve a new medication for the arthritis, but it's complicated apparently." His voice turned bitter. I guess it's been an issue for a long time.

"What about the fibro?"

"There isn't a treatment for fibro. He uses CBD cream when it gets bad, but it doesn't prevent the pain."

"Is he in pain all the time?" I've only known Ezra for two

months, but the thought of him hurting so often made me want to throw one of those apples at the unsuspecting family of four that'd just wandered into our formerly isolated patch.

"A lot of the time . . . Can we talk about something more pleasant?"

I stopped to pick another apple. It was more yellow than red. "Like what?" No bruises on that one either. I put it in my bag.

Lucas picked one, too. "You seem to like your new friends," he said. Across the way, the dad lifted the little girl onto his shoulders.

"Xio isn't a new friend."

"You know what I mean." The girl's brother ran ahead, stopping at a branch he could reach on his tiptoes. He handed the apple to his dad to give to the girl.

"Yeah," I said. "I like them." Zehra and Owen both, but I'm definitely closer to Zehra. Probably because we spend so much time talking in art.

"Are you happy here?"

I thought about it for a moment. It sucked, having to start over, but I do like my new friends and art with Ms. Chang and hanging out in Pride on Wednesdays and hanging out with Ezra. I even don't hate spending time with Lucas. Sometimes. So I told him yes and he grinned at me like I just gave him a million dollars.

"Hey, can we get cider, too?" I asked. There are a lot of things I love about fall, but the drinks are definitely top five. One day, I'd love to live somewhere with fall proper, but Millboro still got cooler this time of year than L.A. did. Zehra insists that they do get proper fall here, but it's still warm enough for short sleeves, so I disagree.

"Of course we can," Lucas said. "Do you want to stop by the pumpkin patch on our way?"

We stayed a few more hours. Lucas wouldn't let me eat any of the apples because, "Pesticides, Avery. We have to wash them first." He did get me cider though, plus a pumpkin-flavored donut that melted in my mouth with every bite. We got a few more to take home to Ezra too.

Ezra was asleep on the couch when we walked in, but stirred when Lucas shut the door. He blinked the sleep out of his eyes. "How was it?" he asked, voice hoarse from disuse. He sat up straighter and positioned his leg awkwardly in front of him.

"Beautiful," Lucas said. He leaned over the couch and kissed Ezra's forehead. "How are you feeling?"

"I'm fine. What did you think?" he asked me.

"You lied," I teased him. "It was mostly couples with kids."

"Avery had an excellent time," Lucas said, gently shoving my shoulder. Honestly, it wasn't bad. At the very least, I got my cider fix.

Ezra yawned behind his hand. "I'm glad," he said, stretching his arms over his head.

"Are you sure you're okay?" Lucas asked again. He put a hand on Ezra's forehead. "You're a little warm."

Ezra shrugged him off. "Did you bring me any apples?" he asked pointedly. "Or are they all for you?" Lucas showed Ezra our haul and I came back to my room to get ready for the fair.

ast night was amazing! Well, rewind a little bit.

The fair ended up being great. I'd never been to a state fair before, like I told Devin, so I didn't know what to expect. We pulled up as the sun was setting and we got an incredible view of the Ferris wheel, highlighted in shining gold and blood red. As soon as we walked in the gates, the smell of fried dough hit my nose and I immediately began salivating.

I was a little taken aback by the sheer amount of plaid at a non-Pride event. I'd opted for a tank top and a light jacket, since it actually did get chilly when the sun went down, but Zehra wore this super cute cropped flannel she got at a thrift store and now I might need one.

Along with corndogs and funnel cake and cotton candy, they

also had what I could only describe as very southern, like hush puppies and deep-fried Oreos. There were loads of rides, everything from a merry-go-round to roller coasters, plus live country music and actual livestock. There were contests for the best cows and pigs in the state and a few contests for plants. "I can't believe you never went to this in L.A.," Zehra said. "My family used to go to this every year."

The big L.A. County fair has local produce and everything, too. I swallowed the sugary threads of my cotton candy and said, "There's too much to do in L.A." Xio nodded in agreement.

Zehra showed me her favorite section, where organizers had set up a display for the best state gourds, and I went on a bunch of the rides with Xio while Zehra got us fried Oreos. She did come with us on the Ferris wheel, though, and we could see the whole town from the top. After, she claimed she hadn't been scared, but she'd clutched my arm the whole time. "It's so high up," Zehra squealed when we teased her.

The lights did look like ants below us and we barely even see the people. "It's okay," I said, still laughing. "You can always hold on to me." Zehra beamed at me and I smiled back.

It wasn't very crowded, but Xio assured me the first and last weekends were pretty rough and Zehra was having a hard time toward the end as it was. She promised she was fine once we got in the car.

Ezra's doing okay again, health-wise. He limped around the house the day after apple picking and the fair and everything. When Lucas asked how he was doing, he insisted it wasn't that bad.

"You're pretty swollen," Lucas said. They were on the couch together, Ezra's leg across Lucas's lap. Lucas had an ice pack wrapped in paper towels pressed to the bloated, too-red skin of Ezra's knee while I did my math homework on the armchair. Lucas only owns a single pair of sweatpants, but he was wearing them then in solidarity with his sick boyfriend. The rest of his casual wardrobe consists of a single black T-shirt, a single white T-shirt, and a Millboro-branded sweatshirt.

"It's better than yesterday," Ezra said, even though it looked the same. I hurt just looking at it. He literally couldn't straighten it all the way. "It's been worse," he added, but if this was 'not that bad,' I can't imagine what 'worse' looked like.

"Can you use the cane? Just for today?"

Ezra rolled his eyes and kissed Lucas quickly, probably to shut him up. "I'm really fine," he said, but I agreed with Lucas for once. There was no reason not to use it except that Ezra likes to pretend he's immune to pain.

"If it's still swollen tomorrow, we should call your doctor."

"It won't be as bad tomorrow," Ezra insisted. He lifted the icepack to check. "The swelling's already gone down." It did get better after that and he hasn't been in pain again since. At least, not that he's said. I'm quickly learning that Ezra saying, "I'm not in pain," could mean anything.

Anyway, back to last night. The last day of the fair was Halloween. But, instead of navigating the crowds, we decided to have our own Halloween celebration at the cemetery across from Zehra's house. Owen tried to convince us we'd get possessed, but he wasn't opposed, so everyone snuck a few beers from their fridges at home and we sat on the mausoleum steps like the first kids to die in a B-rated horror movie.

We were mostly just talking and laughing when a group of guys from our year passed us. "Avery?"

My head snapped up at the sound of Devin's voice. He grinned widely. "Hey," I said. "What are you doing here?" He wore his go-to letterman jacket and a baseball cap and while it wasn't a look I'd normally go for, he rocked it.

"Same as you guys," he said, gesturing to the others. "Can we join you?"

The others looked around at each other and shrugged. I gestured for them to sit with us and my friends all scooted over.

Devin sat next to me and introduced himself and his two friends. "What were you guys doing?" he asked.

"Just hanging out," Owen said. He sat next to one of Devin's friends now on the other side of the circle. The friend grabbed a beer from the middle and cracked it open.

"Do y'all play truth or dare?" Devin asked. Xio and Owen nodded and Devin said, "Do you want to play?"

"Sure," I said quickly.

Devin grinned at me. "Alright then. Truth or dare."

Oh jeez, I hadn't meant to go first. "Truth," I said.

"Do you have a crush on anyone right now?"

Crap. If I opted out, the answer would be super obvious. If I took too long, also obvious. But I didn't want to lie. "Yes," I said quietly.

Devin's friends went, "Ohhh," and Devin's smile widened. "Who?" he asked.

"That's not the game," Xio said loudly. Devin rolled his eyes and I went next. I chose Owen, who chose dare, and he ended up attempting to break into the mausoleum. He failed, but it was hilarious to watch him try.

Owen chose Xio, who chose truth and told us that, no, they hadn't lied about making out with Jaden Frost at a party last year and, yes, it was super gross. I didn't know who Jaden was, but Zehra assured me I wasn't missing out. Xio chose one of Devin's friends and I lost the thread of the game when Devin tapped me on the shoulder. "Want to take a walk with me?" he asked.

My breath caught. "Yeah," I managed, and we both stood. My friends all shot me a collective quizzical look. "We'll be right back," I said, and we were off.

As soon as the others were out of earshot, Devin said. "So, who do you have a crush on?"

I shrugged. Thank God it was dark because I'm sure my cheeks were bright red.

"You know," he said, "I have a little crush on someone too."

Cue me freaking out internally. "Really?" I hoped it was me, but I didn't know. We hadn't spoken in a while, but maybe he was nervous?

"Mmhmm." He stopped walking and turned to me. "Avery Marsh, how would you like to go on a real date with me?"

Yes! Yes! Yes! "I'd like that," I said.

"Great." Devin leaned forward and kissed my cheek and holy crap, not to exaggerate, but it was absolutely magical. My heart was actually pounding. For the record, his lips were *not* chapped like Andy Yu's.

Back at the circle, Devin's friends laughed loudly about something we missed and Zehra looked like she was going to throw up or cry. I felt bad, since I knew how much she hated talking to big groups, especially when she didn't know everyone. But then Devin said, "I think we're heading out." The other guys stood and Devin turned to me and said, "I'll text you."

"Sounds good," I said. They left, and I sat in the circle again.

"Did Devin just ask you out?" Owen asked.

I nodded and instead of freaking with me like I thought would happen, he shot a wary look at Xio. "What?" I asked.

"He has a bit of a reputation," Xio said. "His friends were just talking about how he was screwing around with a junior girl last week."

Oh. "I know that." I don't know why I lied except that I didn't want them to think I didn't know. Besides, we hadn't been going out last week, so Devin was welcome to do whatever he liked.

Owen drove us home not long after that. Lucas and Ezra were on the couch when I walked in and Lucas had his face hidden in his hands, shielding himself from the movie they were watching. It took me a minute to realize that it wasn't a horror movie, but –

"*Coraline?*" I snorted. "You're scared of a children's movie?"

Ezra laughed. "This was our Halloween compromise. Last year's was *Hocus Pocus*."

Lucas looked up. "I'm sorry," he said, "but getting buttons sewn over my eyes sounds horrifying to me."

Ezra kissed the top of his head. "It's not real, love." Something inside my gut twisted. I liked Ezra a lot, but it's always a little strange to see how easy it is for Lucas to be happy with him when we keep missing each other by so much.

I sat on the armchair with my legs over the side. "How was Zehra's?" Lucas asked.

I hadn't told him we were sneaking into the cemetery. Besides, it wasn't like it was actually sneaking. The holes in the bushes around the graveyard were massive. "Fine," I said. "Fun." My heart was still pounding and I could feel Devin's lips against my cheek, and then today in math, when he shot me a wink, I almost died right then and there.

I thought going out with Devin would be the best thing to ever happen to me, but these last two weeks have been . . . off. I mean, Devin is great. We only have math together, but I gave him my schedule and he's been finding me in the hall between classes. We have different lunch periods, but we spend almost every day together after school except Wednesday, which is Pride. I might skip next week, though. Owen will be annoyed, but he'll get over it.

I did ask Devin about the other girl and he said it wasn't a big deal and his friends just like to tease him. I believe him, even if Xio doesn't. I can tell Zehra doesn't like him either. She gets quiet every time I talk about him. Honestly, she's being a little annoying. The other day I asked her if she wanted to join us at the library after school and comb through one of those massive college guides with me and Devin. I pretty much know where I'm applying and started all the applications, but Devin doesn't yet. Anyway, when I asked Zehra to join us she said she had plans even though I knew for a fact that Xio and Owen were both busy after school and her parents were visiting her middle sister at college.

I did see Ms. Chang in the library while we were searching. I told her what we were doing and she asked to see my list. I showed her and she beamed at me. "You'll do amazing at any one of those schools," she said. "I'm a little biased about Purchase. That's where I went, but the others are great, too. Let me know if you ever want to talk about them."

I told her I would and she left. Devin grinned at me. "You're a little bit of a teacher's pet, aren't you?"

I shrugged and busied myself looking at the book, but I wasn't really reading. It's pretty obvious Devin and I are from very different social circles. He's on the football team and I'm in Pride. He's known for sweeping girls off their feet and I'm, well, me. He laughed and said, "Don't be embarrassed. You know I like you, girl."

He keeps doing that, calling me "girl," even though I don't really know how I feel about that label for me. I mentioned that once, but he kept doing it. It's not a big deal and I know that, so I try not to let it get to me when everything else is so good between us. I can't help but think of my parents though, who referred to me as their daughter basically up until I left even though I kept asking them to use "child" or "kid."

Speaking of Mom. It was late by the time we left, so Devin dropped me off at home. I ate dinner with Lucas and Ezra and disappeared into my room to start my homework when Mom's number showed up on my phone.

The phone rang again, but I didn't answer right away. I hadn't heard from Mom since coming here in August except for when I told her I got my stuff and she texted me back like a week later. I took a breath, which reminded me of how Lucas deals with stress or anxiety and picked up the call. "Mom?"

"Hi honey, how are you?"

No acknowledgement of the fact that we haven't heard each other's voices in literal months, but I wasn't surprised. "I'm . . . good," I said. I think I might be losing my only friends here, but "good" works for now. "How are you?"

"You know. Busy." No, I didn't know, because we haven't spoken over the phone in like three months. "What have you been up to? Are you making any new friends?"

"Yeah. I mean, I've been here for a while."

"Of course. Any cute boys?" No mention of anyone but boys either because, of course, she can't deal with the idea I might be interested in anyone else. She'd like Devin, at least. I don't know how I feel about that.

"Not really," I lied.

"That's fine," she said, which, of course it's fine. "I was wondering how you and your brother feel about coming home for the holidays?"

I had forgotten the holidays were coming up. The Thanksgiving holiday is soon and Lucas briefly mentioned cooking something small for the three of us, but we don't have any December break plans. Back in California, I usually spent the week between Christmas and New Year's scrolling on my phone and occasionally hanging out with friends, but we never did anything big. "I'll ask him."

"I'd love to see you."

I wished I could tell her everything. I wished I could talk about Devin and how much I like him and how I love my new friends but I'm annoyed they won't give him a chance and how Lucas and I are mostly fine but it's still so awkward and I hate that because we used to be so close, but Mom and I have never had that kind of relationship, so I said, "I'd like that too," and Mom seemed to take that as agreement to come.

"I'm sure your dad would like to see you too," she said. "Let me know when your break is and I'm happy to chip in for tickets."

"Sure," I said. "I've gotta do my homework."

"No problem. I'll talk to you soon."

"Ok," I said, choosing to believe her. After all, if I see her in December, that would technically be sooner than the last time we spoke. We hung up and I flopped down on the bed and sighed. I would have loved to talk to someone about it and thought about texting Devin, but we hadn't really spoken about my bizarre family situation yet and I didn't want to freak him out. He doesn't even know I'm living with Lucas yet. Xio and Zehra and Owen all knew about my living situation, but I wasn't sure where I stood with any of them. Lucas was out. He and Mom never talk and that would just be awkward. I considered Ezra, but he would probably tell Lucas.

That left no one. I was completely alone.

After weeks of planning, Saturday was Pride's bi-annual trip to DC. As much as Xio and I tried to convince Owen and Ms. Chang that seven o'clock in the morning was too damn early to leave, they wouldn't budge. "We have a packed day," Ms. Chang kept saying, and Owen agreed. I don't know how Zehra felt about it, since we haven't really talked just the two of us since I started going out with Devin. Owen had Xio make schedules for us:

7:30 **a.m.** Departure (ugh)
10 **a.m.** Arrival
10:45 **a.m.** Bayard Rustin talk at the National Museum of African American History & Culture

12 p.m. Lunch at Le Diplomate
1:30 p.m. Explore DuPont Circle
3 p.m. Visit The Dominique Nolan Center
4 p.m. Tour, talk, & treats at Capital Candy Jar
5 p.m. Back on the bus
7:30 p.m. (ish) Return

All that to say, I got up at six, rolled out of bed, and threw on the first sweater and jeans I could get my hands on. Lucas dropped me off and I spotted my friends by the bus. They all had to be there early because they're on the Pride board.

Xio waved me over and I sort of hovered around them while they continued their conversation. This is how it's been since I started dating Devin, me existing around them and them continuing with their lives.

"I'm so excited we're doing the Candy Jar this year," Xio gushed. "I'm stocking up."

"My mom warned me not to buy too much," Owen said sadly. His mom is a dentist.

"Is that really going to stop you?" Xio asked.

"No," Owen said. "I'll just have to eat them all on the bus." Zehra laughed.

No one looked my way after that and soon enough, we got on the bus. I don't know if they're ignoring me because of Devin or what, but honestly, it's getting really old. This was the first Saturday since we got together that Devin and I didn't have a date, but I saw him Sunday to make up for it.

DC is like two and a half hours away, so Xio and I shared a seat and fell asleep while Owen and Zehra talked to Ms. Chang. I woke up when Ms. Chang announced we were ten minutes from the museum. Mouth dry and head fuzzy from my nap, I peered out the window past a sleeping Xio to take it all in.

Pretty much everyone who lives in Virginia has been to DC,

but I've been living in Virginia for five minutes, so this was my first time. It wasn't a city like I'm used to. There were no sky-scraping buildings or anything, but there were a ton of people walking around in everything from spandex shorts to business suits, which, pretty on par with what I know. We drove past the tall gates of the White House (honestly, would have been cooler if we hadn't elected Trump twice) and stopped outside the museum. Xio woke when the bus stopped and we all got out.

We had a bit to stretch our legs and look around before Ms. Chang ushered us into a small lecture hall. A museum worker greeted us as we sat and she launched into her lecture about Bayard Rustin. I'm so mad that I didn't know who he was before. He was super important to the Civil Rights Movement in the sixties, but was shunted to the side because he was gay. He was an activist with gay rights causes in the eighties and did a ton for workers' rights. We don't teach about him now because the U.S. education system is still super homophobic.

More fun facts about Bayard Rustin:

- He was a Quaker, which I still know very little about, but cool.
- He grew up with his maternal grandparents and believed his mom was his older sister for a good chunk of his life. I have no idea what to do with this information, but it's interesting.
- He was one of the lawyers who defended the Scottsboro Boys, who were nine Black teenagers falsely accused of raping two white women in Alabama because racism.
- He was in a musical, which is wildly different than being a lawyer.
- He and his partner weren't allowed to get married in the eighties, so he adopted his partner as an adult

instead so they could have legal protections, which I didn't know you could do until the person giving the lecture said so.

After the museum, we went to a restaurant called Le Diplomate, which is French and gay-owned. Zehra and Owen were talking to Ms. Chang and Xio and I sat a little further down the table with Ty and Carmen, two juniors. We ordered and Ty and Carmen started talking about how the trip was the same or different from when they came their freshman year. Apparently they lobbied our senator that year, but they didn't do the museum tour or have as much time to look around DuPont Circle.

Xio turned to me. "How are things with Devin?" they asked.

The question caught me off guard. "Good," I said. I didn't know how to answer that otherwise. Did they ask me just to be nice? Did they genuinely want to know?

Xio shifted in their seat. "I know we don't love him," Xio said with a nod down the table at Zehra and Owen. "But we do love you. You know that, right? We're still here for you."

That meant a lot to me. "It feels like you guys aren't talking to me because I'm dating him," I admitted.

Xio laughed. Like, head back, loud laughter. I frowned and was about to ask what the hell they were laughing about when they said, "We were just talking about how it felt like *you* weren't talking to *us*."

I had mixed thoughts about that. I didn't love the idea that my friends were talking about me behind my back, even if it was out of concern, and my stomach did a small flip at the idea. But I also had to admit I was glad they weren't icing me out. "Maybe we've been missing each other," I offered. A verbal olive branch.

"Sorry, Avery. I do promise, we still want to talk to you. We all love you."

I felt a little better after talking with Xio. At least my friends didn't all hate me. We left the restaurant for DuPont Circle with promises to Ms. Chang to be back on time and things felt easier with Owen, too, even though we hadn't talked about anything. Maybe it really was two-sided. Whatever it was, I put in a little effort and at the very least I made Owen and Xio laugh at a joke that probably wasn't even funny. Zehra was still pretty quiet, but she could have been overstimulated by everything around us. I decided to give her some grace.

DuPont Circle is a gay gathering point in DC according to both Owen and Google. We tried on some clothes at Secondi, which is a secondhand shop, and there was a cute bookshop we had to drag ourselves out of to meet up with the rest of the group. We gathered outside of The Dominique Nolan Center and the guy who runs the place came out to tell us about the history. Basically, Dominique Nolan was a trans woman who founded the center for kids who don't have a safe space at home. Some of the kids live there and some just spend a lot of time there.

An employee gave us a quick tour of the house-turned-center. Several of the upstairs rooms were still used as bedrooms, most of them with two sets of bunk beds. They were clean and a decent size, but it still made me feel a little funny to know these kids live there. Most of the upstairs was residential, actually, with a small kitchen and a game room, while the downstairs was mostly one large room with all sorts of tables and chairs for the kids to do their homework in, plus a few other rooms like a bigger kitchen and some office spaces. A few of the kids that stayed there full time peered at us from around the corners. I realized with a jolt that a lot of them were our age.

We left and I held my arms around myself. That could be any one of us under different circumstances. If my mom hadn't been able to send me to Lucas, where would I be right now? What if Lucas hadn't taken me in or what if I hadn't had a brother in the first place? I looked up at the group and saw Owen looking at me. He came over and put an arm around my shoulders. "You okay?"

I nodded, but he could clearly see that I wasn't. He ran up to Ms. Chang and told her something I couldn't hear, then he ran back to me and motioned for me to step off to the side with him. We sat on a bench along the sidewalk and Owen said, "You sure you're okay?" I shrugged and bit my lip. "I had a really hard time visiting the center my first time, too," he said. "I'd just come out as trans like a couple months before. I kept thinking about what would've happened if my parents weren't ok with it."

"No, exactly. There's such a thin line between us and those kids at the center."

"There is no line. We could easily be them if things were just a little different."

I nodded. "My mom, she was so upset when I came out to her. She acted like it was just an inconvenience, but I know she was upset. I know that wasn't why she sent me away, but . . ." But also that wasn't *not* why she sent me away. Lucas let it slip recently that she still referred to me as his sister, however many times I asked her not to use that label for me. I brushed it off like it didn't bother me.

Owen's arm found its way around my shoulders again. "I'm sorry. That's really hard."

I sniffed and blinked back tears. "Yeah." He dropped his head onto my shoulder and I put my head on his. "Thanks, Owen."

"Anytime. I love you, you know."

I took his hand and we threaded our fingers together. We stayed like that for a while before we caught up with the others. Owen knew where to go, so we found them at the Capital Candy Jar just as the tour was ending and everyone was marveling at the chocolate. We found Xio and Zehra by a display of white chocolate bars and Xio pulled me aside. "You okay?" they asked. I nodded and they gave my arm a squeeze and showed me the chocolate they'd already collected.

Before we knew it, Ms. Chang was ushering us back onto the bus. Zehra fell asleep on Owen's shoulder in minutes and the rest of us chatted about the chocolates we'd bought and how cool it would be to come back for a weekend, maybe over the summer. I hope Xio and Owen didn't notice how I kept glancing at Zehra. I couldn't help it. Xio said all of them were still here for me, but I don't know. I wished Zehra would say something.

We got in around half past seven, just as Owen planned (he was a little smug about it). Lucas picked me up and we got takeout on the way back. "How was it?" he asked.

It was amazing and devastating and complicated. It was something I still need to sort out in my own head. It was something that, when I tried to tell Devin about it yesterday, his eyes glazed over and I changed the subject and tried to hide how disappointed I was. It made me think about Mom and how lucky I was and how scared I still am. But to Lucas, I said, "It was fine," and changed the radio station.

Texts between Avery and Devin

Tues, Nov 22, 12:03 AM

Devin:
You up?

Me:
yes! what's up?

Devin:
Just thinking about you ;)

Wbu?

Me:
youre so sweet

finishing our math hw

Devin:
Can I ask you a question?

I've been thinking a lot about you calling
yourself nonbinary

What does that actually mean?

Me:
i just don't always feel like a girl

you know?

Devin:
Then why use she?

Me:
i guess i still feel femme? does that make
sense?

Devin:
Not really

Me:
i still feel feminine sometimes, just not "like a
girl"

it's fine if you dont get it

Devin:
It's a little weird, no lie

You still up for my birthday dinner this
weekend?

Me:
yes! im excited:)

Devin:
Me too :)

Devin: Talk tomorrow girl<3

November 26

Devin asked me to spend his birthday weekend with him, so of course I said yes! He's taking me to this super fancy restaurant, so I got a really cute dress with Xio after school this week. We've been pretty ok since DC, but I know they still don't love Devin, so I'm trying to convince them he's a good guy. At the very least, they told Lucas he was nice when Lucas asked them, so I'm grateful for that.

Xio helped me get ready. I'm not *not* confident in my appearance, but even I was blown away by how I looked in this dress. It's silver and shiny and strapless, but it's November, so I have a black sweater I'm wearing over it. Xio said I look hot, so I'm hoping Devin thinks so! He's coming any minute now and I'm so excited!

I'm officially never talking to Devin again. I don't think I've ever been so freaked out in my life as I was on Saturday, which is so upsetting because it started off amazing. Devin picked me up at seven and I managed to convince Lucas that no, they didn't need to meet right then. As soon as I made my escape from the house, we headed straight for the restaurant. I had no idea what to get so he got us both steaks. They were so good, like juicy but also crisp? I don't know. It tasted like rich people food.

We stayed for like three hours just talking and then Devin asked if I wanted to go somewhere to hang out more, so I tried to fight a smile as I said yes. Heat rushed to my cheeks and when he took my hand on our way out, butterflies stirred in my stomach. I don't think I did a very good job hiding my excitement because Devin grinned right back at me and winked.

We got in the car and drove a ways away, until we got to a parking lot I didn't recognize. "Where are we?" I asked.

"We're together," Devin said. "That's all that matters." It was so romantic I wanted to die. He leaned in and kissed me and I basically melted. God, I might throw up just thinking about it.

We made out for while before Devin suggested we get in the back seat. I'm not completely ignorant so I said, "Do you think we can slow down a little?"

"What do you mean?" he asked. I told him I was a virgin and he laughed. "Don't worry, girl. I'll show you what to do."

"I don't know if I'm ready," I said.

He frowned. "What do you mean?"

I thought I'd made myself clear, but apparently not. "I like you a lot," I said. "It's just a big deal for me." I've thought a lot about virginity and what that means, especially as my friends back home started having sex. I know it's an outdated concept or whatever, but I still don't want to regret my first time. The first time Haley had sex, it was with this guy who dumped her the next day and then told all his friends. Those guys all followed her between classes and asked if she'd do them next. We had to go to the principal.

Devin's eyebrows contracted into a sharp V. "Why'd you come out with me then?"

He might as well have slapped me. "I like you a lot," I said again. "I wanted to be with you on your birthday."

"Then be with me," he said. He leaned in again and I pulled away and he jerked back. "What the hell, Avery?"

"I asked if we can slow down," I said again. My voice didn't waiver, but my heart pounded in my chest.

"You're such a tease," he yelled. "Are you kidding me?" He eyed me up and down. "That dress makes you look like a slut by the way."

God, I hoped he couldn't see how upset that made me. "Can you take me home?" I asked quietly. My heart was thudding in my ears and my arms had broken out into goosebumps.

"Find your own way home," he yelled. "Get out of my car."

I had no idea where we were. "What?"

"You heard me. You can walk home." He reached out and grabbed my arm. "If you don't want to be my girlfriend you can get out of my car with that skanky-ass dress."

I tried so hard not to cry. "You're hurting me."

He let me go and I scrambled out of the car. As soon as I shut the door he peeled out and I doubled over, trying to catch my breath. As soon as I'd stopped shaking too hard to make my hands work, I checked my phone so I could call a Lyft. Of course, no signal.

I looked around, but all I saw were woods and this barely lit parking lot that seemed to be in the middle of nowhere. The temperature had dropped several degrees and chills broke out all over my legs.

I took a few more deep breaths and just started walking. After maybe ten minutes I realized I was downtown and pulled out my phone again. I started to open the Lyft app, then I hesitated. Did I really want to get in a car with a strange man after all this? What if something happened?

I called Lucas instead. He picked up right away. "Avery?"

"Can you come get me?" My voice broke and I started crying. "I'm outside the CVS."

"Yeah, of course. The one by the deli?"

"Yeah." I started sobbing. "Lucas, I messed up."

"Ok, it's ok. I'm coming." He said something I couldn't hear and then, "Ezra's coming too, okay?"

"Fine," I said. "Please hurry."

I ducked into the drug store after that to use the bathroom, since anxiety makes my IBS worse, just like stress does for Ezra and his chronic conditions. When I got out, I tried to make myself invisible against the side of the drug store while people walked past, staring at me. I must have smudged all my makeup by now.

Ezra pulled up to the curb five minutes after my call and Lucas got out and I ran into his arms. "It's okay," he said. "You're okay. You're safe." I was shaking too hard to say anything.

In the car, I told them what happened. Lucas was upset, but Ezra was angry. He clenched his jaw so tight I thought he'd never be able to speak. "You're safe now," Lucas kept saying, but I don't know if he was saying it more to me or to himself. At home, Lucas made me hot chocolate and we stayed up until like three in the morning half-talking and half-staring into space. I don't remember most of what we talked about.

Yesterday, I woke up super late and found Lucas and Ezra arguing in the kitchen. "If I were to show up at his house with a bat," Ezra was saying. He was squeezing the chair in front of him so hard I thought the back might snap in half.

"No."

Ezra nodded at me. "I'm not asking you," he said to Lucas.

Lucas glanced at me, too. "I promise you, Avery would rather you not go to prison."

"Just to scare him."

"Jesus, Ezra, no."

"What if I just keyed his car?"

"*No.*" To me he said, "How are you feeling?"

I shrugged. "Fine," I said. Keyed up. Like screaming. Take your pick.

"I'm glad you called last night," Lucas said. "You know you can always —"

"I know," I said. Spare the lecture. I turned to Ezra. "For the record, it's the black Toyota Camry with the license plate that starts KHE. He usually parks it near the gym." Lucas threw up his hands in defeat.

I spent the rest of the day eating junk food and re-watching

Abbott Elementary on Hulu. Lucas made my favorite mac-and-fake-cheese bake and even let us eat dinner in front of the TV. When I got up to get myself more water he took my glass. "I got it," he said.

He kept insisting on waiting on me and it was all ridiculous because Devin didn't actually do anything to me, but it was kind of nice, so I let him. "Thanks," I muttered. He squeezed my shoulder on his way out and for whatever reason that almost made me start sobbing again. I took a breath and refused to look at him or Ezra.

I didn't start my homework until almost eleven and Ezra stayed up with me to do Spanish. "You don't have to," I said.

"I don't mind," he said. "I'm not tired." We both knew that wasn't true. His usual bedtime is like ten o'clock, but I didn't want to be alone, so I let him stay with me until Lucas made us go to bed around one in the morning because Ezra fell asleep at the table.

Today, I sat in the back in math and Devin came storming in yelling about how someone slashed his tires before lunch. He probably thinks it was me, but there's a school full of eyewitnesses saying I was in every class today if he asks. And if Ezra happened to take an extra-long lunch break today, well, maybe I just won't mention it to Lucas.

Prompt: Some students have a background, identity, interest, or talent that is so meaningful they believe their application would be incomplete without it.

I discovered I love to paint when I was five years old. Finger paint, that is. I made a big mess of it. My dad would come home from work most days to find me, my mom, and a good chunk of the table stained red, blue, yellow, and green. As I got older, finger paints became crayons and markers, watercolors, and, most recently, acrylics.

Painting has been a great outlet for me creatively, but also in discovering myself these last few years. I came out as bisexual a few years ago and nonbinary earlier this year and having that creative outlet to express myself has made my transitions so much easier, both because I could turn to painting when everything felt too hard and because painting is fluid in the same way my identities are.

I also moved across the country earlier this year to live with my brother after my parents' divorce, which was hard for me. Having that familiar creative outlet made that change much easier as well, plus it connected me with my current art teacher, Ms. Chang, who has been very supportive both of my creative work and of me as a student.

I have a lot to learn about painting still and I am excited to spend the next four years both improving and studying it. I know very little about the great painters like Frida Kahlo, Andy Warhol, and Mark Rothko, and I think knowing more about them and the history of art can only make my own work better.

December 7

I can't believe I keep thinking about Devin when nothing actually happened. He didn't touch me or anything, but sometimes I have dreams about getting left in the middle of nowhere and not being able to find my way home, or Devin yelling at me and I can't get away from him. I'm always tired in the morning when I have those dreams and Ezra definitely knows something is wrong. The first time it happened he pulled me aside while Lucas was getting dressed for work and asked if I was okay. I told him yes and he said fine, but if I ever needed to talk about anything, we could. He was sweet about it, but I don't even know what I would say.

Besides avoiding Devin in math, things have been going well these last few weeks. I finally submitted all my college apps, though I never want to see another common app prompt as long as I live. Ms. Chang insisted we throw a mini-celebration in Pride for all the seniors. She's super proud of us because she's the best. Even Owen stopped complaining about the lack of Gayla prep happening when she brought out the cupcakes, made with dairy-free butter for us IBS babes.

Toward the end, she asked us about our holiday plans, even though break isn't for a few weeks. Owen is going to his cousins' in New York for Hanukkah. I'm the only other person who's traveling, since Zehra and Xio are celebrating Christmas here. I managed to convince Lucas to come back to California, since he has the week off anyway and I know he'd just spend it watching and re-watching boring classic movies.

Well, not exactly, since Ezra also has the week off. Ezra isn't doing anything for the holidays either, so I keep trying to convince him to come, but he says he won't unless Lucas wants him there. Lucas *does* want Ezra to come, but he keeps making excuses. I keep trying to slip it into conversations. Like the other morning at breakfast they were arguing about the university not having enough money for scholarships. Ezra was going off because, "Economic diversity ultimately helps the school and attracts more students there to later give more money."

"Yes," Lucas said slowly, "but we don't have the money for the scholarships in the first place. Everything we reallocated from last year is going straight into housekeeping salaries and that was enough of a fight as it is."

"You're telling me all the admin need their six figure salaries?"

"No, but we tried with that. They won't give them up."

"Then it's finance's job to look into other funding streams."

Anyway, I jumped in while they were doing their annoying foreplay arguing and said, "Hey Lucas, have you asked Ezra to come home for the holidays yet?"

Lucas's hand twitched. He looked at Ezra. "I –"

Ezra immediately switched from argumentative to supportive boyfriend mode. "There's no pressure," he said quickly. "I'd love to come with you, but I understand."

Lucas nodded and stared down at the table. "I do want you to be there," he said quietly. At least he admitted it.

"I understand," Ezra said again. "Hey Avery, do you think we could let Lucas figure this out on his own?" Fine, whatever, but it would totally be better if Ezra was there. Maybe I'll just keep dropping not-so-subtle hints when Ezra's not around.

Last night, the two of them went to hang out with Jess, formerly of fake girlfriend fame. They asked me to come, or rather, Ezra asked while Lucas did the dishes and pretended he wasn't listening. They trade off who cooks and who cleans sometimes, but since Ezra is objectively the superior chef, Lucas usually does the dishes.

Ezra asked me and I glanced at the back of Lucas's head. "I'm good," I said, more to Lucas than Ezra. If Lucas didn't want me to come, who needed him? Instead, I ordered Indian food on Lucas's credit card and decided to finally clean out the top of my closet. I have plenty of space, but Lucas and Ezra must've been using the shelf as a storage area before and I keep forgetting to tell them to move their crap. I could see the corner of what looked like a floral-pattered box and the edge of something black, but that was it. After my sad, solo dinner, I dragged a kitchen chair into my room and went rummaging. Probably Ezra could've reached the top of the closet without any help, but let's be honest, by the time they got home I would've forgotten again. ADHD, baby.

The box wasn't a box, it turned out, but a floral-print photo album that looked like something I'd find at a grandmother's house, not the home of two men in their mid-twenties. That might be pretty gender-normative, now that I see it in writing. Oops.

There was an actual box, too, dark wood with metal hinges.

A beautiful silver and opal necklace lay inside and I can't say I wasn't tempted to try it on, but I thought I should probably ask whoever the necklace belonged to, especially if it was Ezra's.

The other odd items included Lucas and Ezra's diplomas, a single AmTrack ticket to New York, and a framed photo of a seven or eight-year-old Ezra with a woman who had to be his mother. She was a few shades darker than him with iron gray streaks in her almost black hair, but they had the same smiles, the same bright eyes except that hers were turned down on the corners, almost like her eyes were frowning. The Ezra in the photo hadn't reached his full height yet, but he was already pretty tall based on the doorway in the background. His mom was taller, though surely not anymore.

I set the rest of the items aside and opened the photo album. Four tiny Lucases stared up at me from four different photos, frozen in time at maybe two years old. In one photo, he waved at the camera with one hand while his other gripped a strawberry ice cream cone. In the next, he was perched on the hip of a man with a large mustache probably a few years older than Lucas is now. The man had a cigarette in one hand and held Lucas securely with the other. Lucas's father. Both of them grinned widely. Lucas might have been laughing.

I flipped ahead a few pages. Lucas's dad made another appearance, but he was thinner, his face ashen. It must have been around his diagnosis. He had lung cancer and died pretty quickly, from what little Mom has said about him. Lucas pretty much never talks about him, or maybe he just doesn't talk about him to me. On the opposite page, Lucas was seven and dressed in a miniature tux, his curly hair slicked back. He was adjusting a black bow tie in the mirror and decidedly avoiding the camera with his eyes. His little mouth was pursed in a familiar frown.

Mom and Dad's wedding was featured on the next page. This was before she started dying her hair fifty shades of blonde, so it was dark and wavy and looked a little like mine.

Lucas was hiding in the background of one of the photos, but otherwise it was all Mom and Dad, and then the next page was all me.

I shifted to sit against the wall and balanced the book against my knees. In the first photo on the top left, Mom held me in the hospital, her face pale and sweaty from childbirth. Dad peered over her shoulder with a small smile. The top of his face was cut off by the photo. I couldn't see above his nose.

A few more pages in, I was four and graduating Pre-K. Mom stood to my left, Dad to my right, and Lucas several inches from Dad, his smile frozen and dead-looking and not quite believable. The photo cut off half his arm.

I flipped through another chunk of pages and landed on me at seven or eight-years-old, one of my last ballet recitals before I decided I was too cool for ballet. My parents were always making me do "girly" things, like gymnastics when I was really little and ballet when I was older. I must have gone through a billion leotards. Actually, I remember being not terrible at either, but once I quit I had more time to paint and run around with my friends and not spend hours in front of the mirror pointing my toes. Much preferred.

I scanned for Lucas in any of those photos before I remembered the terrifying drama a few days before the recital. Mom woke me up sometime in the night and said she was taking Lucas to the ER because he couldn't stop throwing up. I couldn't sleep after that and climbed into bed with Dad, but he sent me back to my room, insisting Lucas would be fine and that I was too old to sleep in my parents' room. No one told me if Lucas was okay or if he was even alive until I got home from school that day and they told me it was a bad stomach bug. He was in the hospital for a few days, actually, but Mom and Dad are both in the recital photos, so Lucas must have been out by then, since I can't believe they would have left him alone so sick. The night he came home, I snuck into his room and he let me climb into bed with him and hugged me and told me it was all okay.

The front door opened and present-day Lucas's voice echoed down the hall. "Avery?"

"I'm in my room," I called back. Lucas and Ezra appeared in the doorway and Lucas surveyed the mess with a tight frown. I rolled my eyes. "What?"

Lucas threw up his hands in mock-surrender. "I didn't say anything."

Ezra crouched down next to me and picked up the diplomas. "Hey, you were wondering where these were," he said to Lucas.

Lucas eyed the photo album. "You shouldn't go through other people's things."

Here we go. I stood and put a hand on my hip. "Spare me the lecture, professor. You left this junk in my room, remember?"

"Thanks for getting it down," Ezra said with a sharp look at Lucas. He sat on the floor. "Did you open the box?"

"Yeah," I admitted. "Pretty necklace."

Ezra smiled. "My grandma made it."

"Wait, she made it? That's so cool."

Ezra showed me the necklace again. I sat beside him and when he offered it to me, I took it to get a closer look. He told me about his grandmother and how she made jewelry in Colombia and basically provided for the family for a while with what she got for her pieces. He was about halfway through his story before I realized Lucas had left the room.

December 19

*L*ucas invited Ezra! Ezra is coming! Lucas is still being ridiculous about it and insists on saying Ezra is his friend, but whatever. Apparently when Mom asked why Jess couldn't make it, Lucas said she's going home to her own family. Which is technically true, but like I said, this whole thing is ridiculous.

Ezra's excited. He won't say so, but he lights up whenever we talk about it and he keeps saying how much he wants to see where Lucas grew up, even though he's been to L.A. before. It's pretty sweet, honestly. Lucas is glad too. He's more relaxed now that we've made these plans, though the bar is low. Instead of checking our flight info every five minutes it's more like every twenty.

We never really celebrated the holidays when I was growing up. Dad isn't Jewish, so we never celebrated Hanukkah, and the most we ever did for Christmas is put up a store-bought tree and exchange expensive gifts so Mom could stave off her guilt about being distant from her children the rest of the year.

Sometimes Dad's other kids would come over for a bit, but not usually, especially as we all got older. Now that I don't see Dad every day, I kind of get it. I don't know that I'll be going out of my way to see him when he hasn't made a single attempt to contact me since I moved. This is the first year Mom's expressed any sort of desire to see family for the holidays and I have to assume it's because she doesn't have any family left in the state. Her sister lives in Montana, but they're not close.

Aside from Mom and Dad, I'm also planning on seeing my friends, but that's anxiety-provoking, too. I FaceTimed Vera and Haley a few weeks ago and it was kind of awkward. We hopped on while they were watching *Real Housewives*, which is a show we used to watch after school together because it was on after school, and both of them shrieked their hellos. Vera started telling me all about her new boyfriend and Haley kept jumping in and interrupting because she'd heard the story already and I felt kind of left out.

"What about you and Devin?" Haley finally asked.

Crap, I totally forgot to tell them. "We broke up," I said. "It's totally fine, though."

"Aw, I'm sorry," Vera said while Haley nodded emphatically behind her.

"It's really fine," I lied. "It wasn't meant to be." I wasn't sure why I wasn't telling them what happened. Actually, that's not true. I didn't want to rehash the details, plus it seemed like too much to do over FaceTime. There are over twenty-six hundred miles between Millboro and L.A., and in that moment, I felt every single one of them.

Last night was the first night of Hanukkah, so we did our

own mini-celebration before heading back to California. Lucas put up a menorah. I didn't even realize we had one in the house. He hummed under his breath while he set it up. "That's Beyoncé," I said.

He looked over at me across the candles. "What?"

"What you're humming," I said. "'Love On Top.'"

"Oh. Yes."

How did I ever think this boy was straight? "Remember the song game?" I asked.

"Oh yeah," he said with a small smile. "We'd hum something and the other one of us would guess it."

"Yeah," I said. It wasn't a big deal, but part of me is glad he remembered. Or that I'm not the only one who remembers. He started humming something else and gave me a pointed look. I frowned in confusion for a second before I recognized it. "*Victorious* theme song." I used to beg Lucas to watch it with me after school, ever since he introduced me to the show when I was six or so. Lucas laughed and I smiled.

Presents were uneventful at best. Before we got together to do the exchange, Ezra went out to get a present for himself, which was a tattoo he'd been wanting to get for a while. It's the words "Hope will never be silent" on his torso, which he says is a Harvey Milk quote. I asked him if it hurt and he laughed. "My tattoo artist said people usually hate getting their ribs done. I told her I'm chronically ill. I'm immune to pain." Behind him, Lucas rolled his eyes.

Ezra got Lucas a book by Randa Jarrar because Lucas is a nerd and he wouldn't shut up about this one for a while. Lucas got Ezra this really nice and probably expensive watch that Ezra put on immediately and will probably die in because Lucas gave it to him. They got me a gift card, which is super nice because they didn't have to get me anything at all, and it's not like I have the money to get them something, but I'm still a little hurt, which is also completely nonsensical. It's weird that they know each other so well and they got me something so impersonal. We did a Secret Santa with my friends and Owen got me a great sketchbook, but I wanted something from Lucas and Ezra that proved they knew me better than a roommate. Is that totally selfish of me?

$\mathcal{I}$ didn't realize a person could be literally as "white as a sheet" before watching Lucas get on a plane to California. We'd only been in the air about an hour when the flight attendant stopped in our row to ask if he was okay. He said yes, but as soon as she walked away, his expression went from pleasant but dismissive back to eyes wide, mouth pressed into a thin line, oh-God-I-made-a-terrible-mistake face.

Ezra put a hand on his. "Hey," he said quietly. "What can I do for you?" Lucas shook his head and shut his eyes. As much as I hate to admit it, I get it. I'm anxious about being back here, too. Plus, it's been four months for me, but it's been almost three years for Lucas. Before I moved, I hadn't seen him since before I could legally drive.

During our layover in Denver, Lucas went off to throw up in the bathroom and Ezra pulled me aside. "Does he always get like this with your mom?" I shrugged. When Lucas last visited California, I was fourteen and we didn't spend much time together. Even if he freaked back then, he wouldn't have done it in front of me.

Lucas rejoined us somehow paler than before. Seriously, if he didn't cut that out, he'd be transparent soon. He took his bag from Ezra and forced a big, creepy smile. "Ready?"

I nodded and Ezra took Lucas's hand and whispered something to him I couldn't hear. Lucas shook his head and started off toward our gate.

We were one of the last groups called, so by the time we got to the gate, the flight attendant asked us for our carry-on bags to check because they had run out of overhead bin space. "You'll get them at luggage claim when you get to your final destination."

"What if there's a mistake?" Lucas asked, eyes darting around all the other bags. "Or –"

"It's going to be fine," Ezra murmured. "One more stop."

"The bags are going to be on our flight, right? Under us?" The flight attendant nodded and Lucas gripped the handle of his luggage.

"Sorry," Ezra said to the flight attendant. "He's nervous." He rubbed Lucas's back until, slowly, Lucas pried his fingers from the handle. The woman took his bag with a pained smile.

The second flight was even shorter than the first, but Lucas still had to get up twice to find the bathroom due to anxiety-induced IBS. He squeezed Ezra's hand so tight when we were landing that Ezra's knuckles flashed white too, but he didn't say anything.

Luckily, we had no problems getting our bags, or Lucas might have had a stroke. We got a cab from LAX and drove up to the house in no time. It was a lot bigger than I remembered and, quite frankly, kind of pretentious. An iron gate made its way around most of the property and I couldn't be positive, but I was pretty sure they'd repainted the exterior of the house. It was the same bright white, but it looked fresher than when I left. I half-expected peacocks to be strutting about in the front yard, but of course, birds would have ruined Mom's perfectly manicured grass. I always knew we were wealthy, but I guess I'd never thought about how ostentatious (SAT word I was forced to learn last year) our house was. Ezra stared at it a little too long, but gathered his "Holy crap my boyfriend is rich" thoughts enough to squeeze Lucas's hand one more time before we got out of the cab.

Lucas led the way to the front door. He raised his fist to knock on the ornate wood, then drew his hand back like he'd been burned. He took a deep breath, then knocked twice. There was a pause and then door flew open and there stood Mom, her hair a darker blonde than when I left and a glass of half-drunk wine in her hand. Her face was flushed and her newly dyed hair disheveled. "My kids," she cried. She pulled Lucas into a one-armed hug. "I missed you."

Lucas untangled himself from her embrace. "Hi, Mom."

She turned to me and then it was my turn for an awkward, wine glass-inhibited hug. "You look beautiful," she said. "Virginia agrees with you."

"Thanks," I said, even though I have no idea what that means.

She released me and turned to Ezra. "You must be the friend," she said.

Ezra stuck out a hand. "It's great to meet you, Mrs. Marsh." Mom grabbed his hand and forced Ezra into a final hug. There's no way that wine glass was her first of the day. She's not usually so touchy.

She let Ezra go and ushered us inside. "I have both your rooms ready," she said. "Lucas, I know you said you and your friend could share, but I made up the guest room just in case. Do you want to come see it?"

Lucas looked back at me and Ezra, silently pleading. "I'll come with you," Ezra said.

"Nonsense. Avery can give you the tour," she said with a nod in my direction. She sort of stumbled over my name, like it tasted unnatural in her mouth, but at least she didn't deadname me. A big improvement for her. She took Lucas by the wrist and dragged him up the stairs, and I gave Ezra a quick tour of downstairs, which had more rooms than Lucas and Ezra had in their whole house, including a second living room, an office, and dining room. We ended up in the first living room, which is at least twice the size of Lucas and Ezra's. Ezra sat on the white leather couch. "It's a beautiful house," he said.

"Yeah." I almost thanked him until I remembered I don't live here anymore.

Ezra gave me a small smile. "Do you want to take bets on how long it takes your mom to admit she can't remember my name?"

I couldn't help but laugh. "Don't take it personally. She called Xio Alex the entire time we were friends." As kids, I meant. I don't think I even told her Xio would be at my new school.

"How long before we rescue your brother?"

"He'll come back down eventually," I said, but they'd already been gone for ten minutes. What could they possibly be talking about for so long? Ezra looked back toward the doorway, but didn't say anything. "Are you out to your parents?" I asked.

He turned back to me. "My mom died when I was twelve," Ezra said. He flashed the semicolon tattoo at me and said, "This one was for her."

My stomach lurched. I knew a lot of people who had or wanted semicolon tattoos for mental health. It symbolized continuing on, that your story isn't over. It was usually for someone who'd been depressed or suicidal. I hadn't thought about it when Ezra first showed it to me. "What about your dad?" I asked quietly.

"My step-dad died last year, but he got to meet Lucas." He smiled and said, "Actually, my grandma adores Lucas. She's constantly asking why we haven't gotten married yet."

"Is this the jewelry-maker grandma?" Ezra nodded and I asked, "She didn't want to see you for the holidays?"

"She lives in Italy," Ezra said. "We went last year for the holidays, actually, but it's expensive to go every year."

"She lives in Italy?"

"Mmhmm. My mom was born in Colombia and lived in Italy until I was born and then she came to the U.S."

"Ok, that is so cool," I said. "Do you speak Italian too?" Everything I learn about Ezra makes me question why he's with Lucas instead of someone wildly more interesting.

He replied with something in Italian and I told him, "I have no idea what you just said, but I'll take that as a yes." He laughed.

At last, Lucas and Mom joined us in the living room. Mom still had that creepy plastic smile plastered on her face and it made me want to throw something. He still hadn't come out to her, or else she wouldn't be nearly so fake-cheerful. Lucas looked close to passing out. "Well," Mom said. "Why doesn't everyone put their bags away? Dinner will be ready in an hour."

We headed upstairs together and split off to drop our bags in our rooms. Mine looked pretty much the same as when I left. The shelves Dad put up just three years ago still had some of the stuff I hadn't packed, like a few schoolbooks and a seashell Lucas found on the beach once and gave to me when we were little. The walls were the same pale lavender I'd never liked and Mom had apparently bought a copy of my old sheets, because my bed looked the same, too. I shouldn't be surprised. In the seven or eight years since Lucas left, his room had never changed either. I used to sit in there when I wanted a change of scene, especially since his room had a desk in it and mine didn't.

The bookshelves stayed full of eighteen-year-old Lucas' books and the top dresser remained home to a large photo of him, me, Mom, and Dad on a trip to Vancouver when I was maybe six. I wondered if he'd take it down this time.

I suppose dinner is now, since Mom said "ready in an hour" about an hour ago. Let's see if I can trick Mom into admitting she doesn't know Ezra's name.

The rest of the trip went about as well as expected. Mom asked me that first night if I was "still doing the pronoun thing" and I blew up at her, which killed any illusion that we were one big, happy family. I stormed off to my room and I heard Ezra behind me trying to explain nonbinary gender to my dear mother. A valiant effort on his part, but she'll never get it. Later, Lucas came to check on me. I told him I was fine and rejoined the family for Monopoly and Mom pretended like the whole interaction hadn't happened. Lucas won the game. He probably needed to win something.

It took me three days before I called Mom out for not actually knowing Ezra's name. The four of us were gathered around the fireplace, all wearing oversized sweaters and pajama pants. Lucas pulled a blanket over his and Ezra's legs. "Are you warm enough?" he asked quietly. It wasn't particularly chilly, but Ezra's always cold. His hands are ice all the time, so it's a valid question. It's an arthritis thing, he says.

"I'm fine," he said with a small smile. I could tell he wanted to reach out and take Lucas's hand or give him a quick kiss, but sitting under the blankets together would have to do for now. I felt bad for Ezra. It must suck to be a secret. As it was, their legs were very obviously touching under the blanket the whole time.

"Your friend knows he can ask for more blankets if he wants them," Mom said, like she and Ezra were best friends even though she'd known him for all of five minutes. She had yet another glass of wine in her hand, this time white. Mom and Lucas both drank way too much the whole trip. Thank God Ezra was there because if he hadn't been, either Mom and I would have killed each other or Lucas would have died of alcohol poisoning.

Anyway, that was when I said, "You keep calling him, 'your friend.' Do you even know his name?"

Lucas went very still. Mom scoffed. "Of course I do."

"Really?" I asked. "What is it?" A beat of silence. Lucas scratched his nose and reached for the wine. Mom didn't know how to answer.

Naturally, she was angry with me about that for the rest of the week.

Overall, Mom seemed to like Ezra, which made the whole thing so much more surreal. She told me once when Lucas and Ezra had gone to bed that Ezra would be, "A very attractive young man if he didn't have those tattoos on his arms."

We were in the kitchen together drinking hot chocolate. I was torn between telling her about the other two tattoos and fighting pure revulsion re: Mom referring to Lucas's boyfriend as "attractive." I shrugged.

"Does he have a girlfriend?" I shrugged again and she said, "What's Lucas's girlfriend like? Jess?"

"Oh. She's nice." I hadn't actually met Jess in person yet.

Mom pursed her lips. "I would've liked to meet her," she said. God, she was either that obtuse or just really, really wanted Lucas to be straight. Maybe both. I finished my hot chocolate and got myself out of there.

Lucas and Ezra didn't act all couple-y while we were there, but there were a few times Mom left the room and Ezra whispered something that made Lucas smile or Lucas would bury his face in Ezra's shoulder for a second, like he was taking a break from the world. They're actually pretty sweet together. Kind of couple goals. I still have no idea what Ezra sees in Lucas, but you know what, it's not my problem if he wants to spend his life with my high-strung disaster of a brother.

Dad came by after a couple days, so I got to see him. Lucas decided to give Ezra a tour of the city that day, which he probably did on purpose. Lucas and Dad have never gotten along. That sucked though, since showing Ezra around the city would have been a lot more fun than pretending to be excited about seeing Dad while he pretended to care about what I've been up to at school. He came by the house and he and Mom didn't act any differently than they have the last decade, which was fine but also kind of strange. I guess they've been mentally divorced for a lot longer than they've been legally divorced.

Mom pretended like she had something vague and unspecific to do out of the house, so Dad and I sat on opposite ends of the leather living room sofa, avoiding eye contact. Did he feel guilty? Or did he just not know how to talk to his queer, nonbinary kid? At last he asked, "How are things?"

I shrugged. "Fine," I said.

"You looking at colleges?" More gray streaked his thinning ginger hair since the last time I saw him.

"I applied. I'm going to art school next year." He grunted his disapproval and I pretended like I didn't notice. That was pretty much the highlight of our time together. Mom came back after about an hour and Dad made an excuse to leave.

I got to see a few of my friends for New Year's, but that was weird, too. Vera had these red highlights that looked totally great on her, but it was strange to see such a stark change. Maybe I didn't notice it on the FaceTime because she tied her hair back. Haley got her nose pierced over the holiday, so I didn't feel as out of the loop about that one, since everyone else was freaking out about it, too, but they all have stories from this year I'm not a part of and I've grown so much in the last few months. I tried explaining my new friends and most of them know Xio, but none of them really got how great it was to have such a queer group of friends or how my new friends make me feel so seen. "That's cool," Haley said. "Oh! Did you hear about Andy Yu? He's dating Maggie Nagoski now. Have you heard from him at all?" I smiled and nodded and pretended not to be bothered by the fact that she'd changed the topic to yet another thing I didn't really care about.

I tried to say more, but when I mentioned it was awesome that we all did Pride together, Vera said, "Yeah, you'd need it in Virginia," even though Millboro is pretty liberal. Like they do a Pride parade over the summer, even though it's in August for whatever reason. I probably would have thought the same if I had never gone there, though, and this probably would have happened when we all went to college anyway, the whole us not getting each other thing, but then it would have been all of us with new lives and not just me. I got back to the house around one in the morning and Mom and Lucas and Ezra had already gone to bed.

Needless to say, it's nice to be back. Lucas is a lot calmer and it was great to see my friends. Owen is freaking out now that it's officially the year of the Gayla and we teased him about said freak out at lunch. I felt a little bad after a while, but Zehra kept laughing and she has a smile like sunshine, so sorry, Owen, but it was totally worth it.

85

From: lucas.wilde@gmail.com
To: daphnelawrence@hotmail.com
Subject: Hello there!

Dear Daphne,

I was so sorry to miss you in LA! It sounds like you had an amazing time with Wes's family in Spain, though, so I can't be too sorry. A little jealous, to tell you the truth. I'll be living vicariously through your photos as soon as you post them on Facebook.

Things with Avery have been fine. I know she's hurting about everything happening with our mom and her dad and I wish I could provide her with more guidance. I can't imagine having to do my last year of high school in an entirely new town. Truthfully, though, they've been doing wonderfully academically and they've made some fantastic friends. Did you know the Sotos when they lived in LA? I think I told you how Mrs. Soto was the one who referred me to my job at Millboro when I was applying after grad school. Their oldest kid, Xio, was Avery's best friend in elementary school and they're at the same school again for their senior year.

My mom was about as expected. She kept asking after Jess and told me more than once she didn't understand why Avery insisted on being called, well, her name, which of course upset Avery. Ezra was there as well, as a friend, so again, about as well as expected. He was great, of course, and it was so amazing to have him there, but I kept thinking my mom would realize we were together and kick us out. I know that's illogical, but it was definitely in the back of my mind the whole time we were there.

Otherwise, Ezra has been doing alright. Work is going well and he's been amazing with Avery. His meds aren't working particularly well, though, so he's been fighting with the insurance company, but hopefully they put him on something effective soon. He doesn't like to talk about it, but I know he's in pain and I wish I could do more.

Anyway, happier news! You're getting married so soon! I'm excited to hear more about your trip in your next email and can't wait to see you in less than a year for the ceremony! I'm beyond excited for a reunion and to travel out to San Francisco next fall. Say hello to Wes for me.

All my love,

Lucas

$\mathcal{B}$reaking news. Major news. Sort of wonderful but potentially life-wrecking news.

Actually, rewind. This all started because in addition to a Polaroid camera from their parents, a really soft sweater from their grandparents, and an incredibly cute undercut, Xio's little sister gave them a really gross cold over the holidays that Xio then gave to me and Zehra the first week back, so I spent that weekend basically dying in my room and texting Zehra about our shared plight.

Zehra:
I think Ive used a billion tissues by now :(

> **Me:**
> same. i can't breeeeeathe

I set my phone aside to grab a tissue and blow my nose in the hopes I'd be able to breathe just a little bit. No such luck. I could hear Ezra coughing down the hall, since I got him sick with Xio's cold over the weekend too (I feel terrible about that, especially since his arthritis flared up because of it). The whole house was basically a petri dish.

I tossed the tissue into the trash can and checked my phone. Zehra hadn't responded, so I texted her again.

> **Me:**
> if i die you can have my books

> **Zehra:**
> lol
>
> Pls don't die!

> **Me:**
> no promises!

Anyway, that Tuesday Owen was working on a group project in the library and Xio was making up a test from the week before, so Zehra and I ate lunch together. I love it when it's the four of us, but there's something different about just me and Zehra. She's so funny and she just gets me. I told her about feeling weird with my old friends and we talked about social anxiety and how that makes everything about a billion times worse. Plus, on top of regular anxiety, there's college acceptance anxiety now and that's *actually* the worst. "My biggest fear is that I don't get in anywhere," Zehra said.

"My biggest fear is that everyone else gets in everywhere and I get all rejections back."

"Right? I totally have nightmares about it."

"You'll get in though," I said. "You're so smart." My grades were okay, but I was always a little self-conscious when Xio finished an English test ten minutes before me or Zehra worried a B+ would screw up her GPA.

Zehra shook her head. "I hate waiting."

"Have you been up to Mass yet?" Pretty much all of Zehra's schools were in Massachusetts, in or around Boston. Her cousins all lived there and she grew up going there for holidays, plus Boston is a big college city. Xio's schools were all in Virginia and Owen's were all within a four-hour radius. I was the only one of us applying to schools all over the country.

"I looked at all my schools last summer. I really loved Hampshire, but I don't want to jinx it."

"You'll get in," I said, and Zehra beamed at me.

The bell rang, startling us both. We gathered the remnants of our caf salad (me) and egg salad sandwich (Zehra, who almost always had the same thing) so we could beat the rush. We started off down the hall together and she said, "Want to come over later? I think Xio's busy today."

I nodded. "That sounds great," I said. We walked to her house after school and watched *Wicked* on her laptop, since Zehra had never seen it. We didn't do much talking, but it was a comfortable, easy silence. It felt familiar, even though I haven't known Zehra that long.

I got home around six that night and found Lucas and Ezra on the couch under a hundred blankets. It was Lucas's turn to sleep all day and use about a thousand tissues and drink a crapload of ginger tea because it was Ezra's favorite and we always had some in the house. Plus, like me, his IBS acts up when he's sick, so it kept him from feeling too nauseated. I felt less bad about Lucas being sick because he probably got it from Ezra, not me. Besides, if we were going to trace it all the way back, it was Xio's sister who got us all sick in the first place.

Lucas looked up at me with glazed eyes. "Where were you?"

he asked. His voice sounded like someone took it and ran it through a blender. I couldn't see his legs under all the blankets, but I'd bet his single pair of sweatpants had made an appearance.

"At Zehra's," I said. "Is that a crime?"

"You could have text . . ." He trailed off halfway through the word, grabbed a tissue from the box on the coffee table, and sneezed loudly three times in a row. I am so, so glad that isn't me anymore.

"You can save the lecture for when you're capable of staying awake for more than four hours at a time," Ezra said gently. He was a little congested and his voice sounded scratchy still. His meds mess with his immune system, so every time he gets sick, it takes him twice as long to get over it would for me or Lucas. His knee was braced from the accompanying flare up. He didn't sound as terrible as Lucas at least, who groaned and lay back against a mountain of pillows. Ezra half-laughed, half-coughed. "You're adorable."

"I'm not adorable," Lucas whined. "I'm sick." He grabbed another tissue and coughed into it.

"Adorable and sick," Ezra said. Lucas blew his nose and pouted.

After that, I went to Zehra's every day after school, including after Pride on Wednesday. On Friday she took me to the skating rink the next town over. One of her sisters was still home from college for the holidays, so Zehra took her car. It wasn't busy right after school, which we both prefer, so we had the whole rink to ourselves.

"I used to be obsessed with skating," Zehra told me while we were lacing up her skates. "I wouldn't stop talking about the winter Olympics. My parents could probably still list all the songs they used in 2014."

"My dad used to watch the Olympics every time, but he always wanted to watch the 'real sports,'" I said with exaggerated air quotes. "My brother used to love the skating and Dad would always change it." Thinking about that now, it's a miracle I didn't suspect Lucas was gay years ago. Johnny Weir was his actual hero.

Zehra pulled a face. "He's missing out." She stood and held out a hand. "C'mon. I'll help you."

I didn't say I actually used to skate with friends back in California or that I wasn't worried about falling. If I did that, I wouldn't have a reason to hold Zehra's hand and that was something I realized I wanted very much. It was soft and warm and nearly the same size as mine and I had a bad feeling the chills up and down my arm weren't from the weather. We talked while we skated and Zehra showed off some moves. She info dumped a bunch about skating and I learned a lot, like:

- The London Olympic Games first had figure skating in 1908.
- It used to be that none of the songs they play during Olympic competitions were allowed to have lyrics. I didn't ask Zehra why, but I'm sure she would know. Now I'm curious, damn it.
- In 2015, Olivia Oliver set the record for spinning the fastest of any skater by turning three hundred and forty-two times per minute.
- Someone invented metal blades around the thirteenth century. Before that, people used animal bones (ick).
- The Zamboni that goes out and smooths out the ice every few hours actually uses hot water, which doesn't seem to make sense, but Zehra assured me it's true. Ice is too brittle to skate on after it gets below a certain temperature.

A little after five, parents started showing up with their

young kids, so we moved to the coffee shop next door. We both got hot chocolate and sat by the window overlooking the street.

My favorite thing about sitting by the window is people watching. I told Zehra this and she asked if I made up any stories. I didn't usually, but I told her I could try. I pointed to the young woman walking by on her phone and said, "She's on the phone with her employee. They're having an affair and the secretary just found out and they're trying to figure out how to keep it under wraps." Zehra laughed and urged me on and I pointed to a young boy and a woman holding his hand across the street. "She just found out her son isn't actually her biological kid. It's a switched at birth stitch. She's trying to figure out how to tell him." Zehra laughed again and her whole face lit up and I found myself wondering what it would be like to kiss her.

So that's my big problem. I have a not-so-small crush on one of my only friends on the entire east coast and telling her would completely wreck our relationship, plus my friendships with Xio and Owen if I make things awkward with them, too. Like, they were Zehra's friends first and I know they love me, but if they had to pick one of us, I know it'd be Zehra. It's not like I can talk to Xio or Owen about it either because let's face it, I don't trust either of them not to laugh in my face for developing an incredibly inconvenient crush on one of my best friends. They would laugh in a loving way of course, but still. I'd be screaming about it right now if Lucas and Ezra weren't right down the hall.

Because it's senior year and because my parents decided parenting wasn't for them, I'm stuck prom shopping tomorrow with my older brother, which would be fine if Ezra could come because Ezra has a sense of style that isn't college-professor-in-the-1980s. Alas, Ezra has plans this weekend with his coworkers, so I'm stuck shopping with the only gay man on the planet who acts like the mall is the cave of terrors from *Indiana Jones*. Or the cave of whatever it is. I haven't actually seen the movies.

I'm low-key nervous about it too because I don't know yet if I want a dress or a tux or what, which shouldn't be a big deal, but it is. I like wearing dresses, but I always feel like they make me look super girly. I mean, the whole point of them is to be a little girly. I know in my head that wearing a dress doesn't make me any less nonbinary, but I can't help but be super self-conscious about it.

Ugh. I hate everything.

Ok, prom shopping with Lucas wasn't ideal, but not nearly as terrible as I thought it would be. First, he was super understanding about me wanting to try on dresses and tuxes and all my gender dysphoria around that. I told him I was feeling off about it yesterday and it turns out he took like an hour that night to search the best stores to buy prom outfits of all kinds and cross referenced them with the stores we have at our mall. Ezra told me at breakfast this morning. That's honestly big brother goals.

We started at Macy's because they have all kinds of outfits and after like half an hour of looking, I went into the changing room with a bunch of options. The first dress I tried on was short and black and tight enough that I felt my organs squeezing together, so I nixed that one. Then I tried this sparkly, sequined tux that might work for the Gayla, but not for prom. Plus, the fabric was scratchy as hell.

My third option was a long, dark red, strapless dress that I didn't hate and didn't have any of the aforementioned issues, so I went out to show Lucas and found him talking to a woman around his age with long, braided cornrows and two shopping bags dangling off each arm. His eyes darted frantically around the room for an escape. She had her hand on his bicep and giggled too loudly at something he must've just said.

I swallowed a laugh at his expense and marched over. "He's gay," I said, "but good try."

The woman didn't even look embarrassed. "All the good-looking guys seem to be." She sighed and gathered her bags. "Well, have a great day, Ernest."

Once she was out of earshot, I snorted. "Ernest? You gave her a fake name and you couldn't think of anything better than Ernest?"

"I panicked," Lucas hissed. His whole face was tomato red. I'm laughing just remembering this.

"Maybe she didn't know you're gay because you're sitting here acting like Macy's is your own personal torture chamber."

"The 'gay men love shopping' thing is a horrible stereotype," Lucas muttered. "What did you need?"

I gestured to the dress. "Uh, hello? Thoughts?"

He barely glanced at it. "Looks nice."

I rolled my eyes and started back toward the dressing room. "I'm texting a picture to my friends."

After that, I tried on a few more things and then we went up to the food court to refuel while I thought about my options. At the food court, I got a hot dog with a twisty pretzel bun and Lucas got a salad. We sat and I asked, "Did you go to your prom? I don't remember."

Lucas nodded and swallowed a mouthful of lunch. "Do you

remember my friend Daphne?" I nodded. She was one of Lucas's best friends and I'm pretty sure I remember her always having different hair colors. Lucas continued, "She liked me. A friend told me. It wasn't fair to her, but . . . I asked her and she said yes."

"Poor girl."

Lucas took another bite. Chewed. Swallowed. "We laugh about it now," he said. "But the night of she tried to kiss me. God, that was a disaster."

I laughed. "You must've been bright red," I teased. I pictured Lucas the way he'd been in Macy's earlier, but my age and in a slightly-too-big tux.

"Definitely," he said. "I think she got together with her current fiancé later that night, though, and I made out with the quarterback in the bathroom, so win-win."

We were both laughing now, hard and breathless. It took us a minute to calm down, and then we looked at each other and started laughing all over again. "Damn," I said when I finally caught my breath. "You were wild, Lucas."

"I don't know about that," he said, but he was grinning. "C'mon, we've got to finish lunch or we'll never find you an outfit."

We didn't end up finding anything for me today, but I did get a new coat plus some idea of what I might like. I do think I want a dress, which I almost talked myself out of again until Lucas gave me a whole lecture in the middle of the store about how I can be nonbinary however I want to be. It was super cheesy and also very sweet.

Valentine's Day is right around the corner and there's no reason that should stress me out as much as it does considering I've never had a Valentine's date in my life and we're all going together to the Gayla anyway, including Owen and his boyfriend, but here we are. It's less stressful to think about that than college acceptances coming next month, so I'm picking my battles.

In non-romance romance news, Zehra and I hung out almost every day last week and I'm positive she knows about my super embarrassing crush on her and is desperately trying to find a way to let me down easy. Yesterday, we spent hours just walking around the school track and talking about our top choices for schools. I like the idea of going back to a city, even if it's not huge like L.A. We're both looking at small schools in general, me because most art schools are small and Zehra because she doesn't think she'd do well at a big school.

In theory, I should love spending time with Zehra. I *do* love spending time with Zehra. It also makes me more anxious than the time in tenth grade when we had to write our own poems for English and recite them for the class. I ended up pulling an IBS version of *The Princess Diaries* and ran out of the room.

Today was especially rough because Owen and I ran into Devin making out with his new girlfriend in the hall on our way to Spanish. Owen pushed past them (harder than he needed to, but I wasn't complaining) and we made it to class on time. He asked me if I was okay and I lied and said yes even though I was furious. I don't want to be with Devin anymore, but it's so unfair that he has someone already while I have an annoying crush on one of my only friends.

Owen had band practice, Xio had to babysit their younger sister, and Zehra was visiting her dad's parents about an hour away, so I was the only one without after school plans. I took the bus home alone and flopped down on the couch and buried my head in a pillow and screamed.

Ezra poked his head around the corner. "Everything ok?"

I sat up too quickly and sent the pillow flying. "What are you doing here?" Ezra didn't get off work most days until half past four.

"I live here." Briefly, I worried he might be sick again. Ezra does these injections every other week for the arthritis. The first time I found out about them, I'd walked in late from hanging out with my friends one night and saw him in the kitchen, icing his leg to numb it before he had to stab it with a needle. A few days later, he showed me the massive greenish-yellow bruise on his thigh.

Anyway, last week his meds caused a migraine that lasted like two days and he couldn't move, so he had to miss a day of work and worked from home for two days after that. The worst part about that is the drugs only sort of work for the arthritis anyway, so he's been fighting with his medical insurance to get better meds.

He's sick half the time from the treatment and it sucks, plus the actual chronic illnesses, so it's fair that I jumped to worst-case scenario, but then he said, "Also, the plumbing at the office broke and they're letting us work from home."

"Ah." Cool, now I embarrassed myself in front of Ezra.

He came over and tapped my knee with one finger. I rolled my eyes and moved over. Ezra sat next to me and said, "You know, I didn't expect to see you here until six or seven either."

I sighed. "Everyone's busy," I said.

"Is everyone being busy the reason that pillow is on the floor?"

Ezra wouldn't relent and I was so sick of trying to keep it all to myself, so I told him. I told him about Zehra and spending time together and seeing Devin in the hallway and how it's not like I need a partner but I really like Zehra but it would ruin my friendships and seeing Devin in math sucks because I constantly have to remember what how hung up I was on him and college acceptances are coming soon but what if I don't get any because there are so many people out there who are better than me and —

Ezra held up a hand. "Take a breath."

I nodded and toyed with my hair. "Sorry." He probably thought it was one little thing and there I was spilling everything I've done every second for the last month.

"Don't be sorry." I tucked my hair behind my ear and he said, "Let's start with college acceptances, ok? You are so incredibly talented, Avery, and anywhere would be lucky to have you. If, worst case scenario, not a single school can see that, which I doubt will happen, you'll stay here with us and try again."

"But everyone else will be going to college."

"Every other seventeen-year-old applying for colleges this year is in the same boat. And there is literally nothing you can do about it until next month. I know not stressing is easier said than done."

"No, you're right." He was also right that it was easier said than done, but college acceptances were too big a thing to deal with right now. "What's number two?"

"It's not a bad thing to like Zehra. She sounds wonderful and it sounds like she cares a lot about you in one way or another. Maybe it wouldn't hurt to give her a chance."

I went quiet for a moment. The thought of putting myself out there and getting rejected was so completely terrifying I didn't know if I could even consider it. "Is there a three?" I asked.

He nodded. "We never really talked about what happened in November with Devin."

I bit my lip and looked away. "I mean, nothing happened. We didn't *do* anything."

"I know that. Please tell me to stop if you want me to, but it sounds like it was a very scary experience for you."

It *was* scary, but I felt ridiculous saying so. "He didn't do anything though. He didn't touch me."

"That isn't the only way he could have hurt you." I shrugged and he said, "Have you ever considered therapy?"

"I don't need therapy for that." Not that therapy was bad. I knew a ton of people doing it. Zehra and Owen both did therapy. For Devin, though? Things happened to other people all the time that were so much worse.

"It's not a contest," Ezra said, because I swear between me and Lucas that guy is a mind reader sometimes. "Just because he didn't physically hurt you doesn't mean you don't need to talk about it." I didn't answer, so Ezra continued, "I see a lot of people at the crisis center who've had things happen to them you'd probably consider awful and so many of them 'not that bad' themselves."

"Hmm."

"Plus, if my parents got a divorce and I moved across the country my senior year of high school, I might need to talk about it sometimes too."

"Lucas would freak if I told him I wanted to see a therapist about Devin." He freaks out when someone gets a paper cut, let alone admits to psychological trauma.

"Lucas . . . would understand better than you think."

"What do you mean?"

Ezra pressed his lips into a thin line. Then he said, "Therapy probably saved my life. After my mom died, I got reckless. I was doing a lot of crap that probably would've gotten me killed eventually. My step-dad put me in therapy. I hated it. Now every time something big comes up, I can't wait to tell my therapist."

"I didn't know you were in therapy," I said quietly.

"I am. We can talk about that too if you want."

I shook my head. "Thanks for . . . thanks." Something about Ezra talking to me at all made me feel better in the moment. I don't know. It's nice to know there's a single adult in my life who cares about me.

"Think about it," Ezra said. A wicked grin spread over his face and he said, "Now, tell me more about Zehra." I groaned, but Ezra went on. "Is she cute?"

"So cute." I pulled up an Instagram photo and showed it to him. It was selfie of her and Owen from a few months ago, when she was distracting him before his surprise party. How had I not realized then how adorable she was? Probably because I was so obsessed with Devin.

"Totally in your league," Ezra assured me. I don't believe him, but it was nice to hear. At least by the time Lucas got home, I didn't feel like screaming anymore.

*E*zra didn't tell us where he was taking us, just told us to get dressed and get in the car by noon. Of course, Lucas was ready fifteen minutes early and gave me the stink eye for being five minutes late, but Ezra didn't care, so I ignored him. We drove for a while until we stopped outside the local park. "What are we doing here?" Lucas asked.

Ezra put a finger to his lips and got out of the car. We followed him to the entryway, where Ezra pointed up at a flyer with a turquoise background and two photos, one of a group of smiley volunteers and one of a litter of puppies. The flyer read:

Starting February, The Millboro Makers will host our monthly popup festivals at Millboro Central Park! This month, we have dozens of vendors, local artists and food and beverage trucks, plus we've partnered with The Millboro Animal Society to bring in a bunch of adoptable furry friends. Vendors, see the link below for future events.

Lucas finished reading the sign and turned back to Ezra with his arms crossed. "We are not getting a puppy."

Ezra laughed. "No, but we can play with them." Lucas arched an eyebrow and Ezra said, "Look, both of you need to take a day to relax."

Lucas and I made awkward eye contact. I didn't think Lucas was any more stressed out than normal, considering his baseline was freaked, but Ezra would know better. He put an arm around Lucas's waist and said softly, "It won't hurt you to take a breath for one afternoon."

I started off toward the field. "I'm going to find the puppies," I said. Lucas shot Ezra another exasperated look as I passed them, but they did follow me. We found the dog people and they let us into one of the pens with three lab puppies, two cocker spaniels, and two schnauzer-poodle mixes who were absolutely adorable. Ezra got on the grass with me and Lucas glanced over his shoulder before joining us on the ground.

The volunteer from the animal place headed over to us. "Are you looking to adopt?"

"Looking to de-stress," Ezra told her before Lucas could protest. "Have you gotten a lot of people so far?"

The woman chatted with Ezra and I took out my phone to send my friends pics of the puppies. All of them texted back immediately.

Zehra:
OMG where r u!?

Xio:
Puppies!!!

Owen:
Those are so cute i want to die holy crap

I told them I was at the park and put my phone away just as the woman brought out an older standard schnauzer. "Everyone's excited about the puppies," she said. "We have half a dozen adoption applications for each of them, but no one wants to adopt poor Frida."

Lucas scratched her behind the ears. "How old is she?" Frida laid down and rested her head on Lucas' knee.

"Five and she's spayed now, but people want puppies. They want to raise them."

Ezra glanced at the dog, then back at Lucas with a small smile. "You said you didn't want a puppy, but . . ." Lucas glared at him.

We hung out with Frida and the puppies for a while longer before we headed over to the food trucks. It smelled like the fair, all fried food and sugary sweets. We all got falafel and sat at one of the picnic benches. Ezra was on his phone the whole time, which wasn't like him. Lucas peered over at him. "Everything ok?"

"Yes, yes, sorry." He put it away. "Remember how Jess has been looking for the perfect dog for forever?" Lucas nodded and Ezra said, "I just texted her. She's on her way to meet Frida."

I thought Lucas would groan or roll his eyes, but he just laughed. "You're incorrigible," he said. Ezra grinned like it was a compliment and took a bite of his sandwich.

We stayed for maybe an hour and listened to the bluegrass band a few feet to the left and the shrieking children on the playground up ahead. Jess ended up coming by with Frida on a leash and a bag full of dog things as we got up. Lucas and Ezra greeted her with hugs. "How are you?" she asked Ezra. "I haven't seen you in forever!"

Ezra grinned. "I'm good. I'm glad everything worked out." He pat Frida on the back.

"Oh my God, thank you for texting me. She's honestly perfect."

They caught up for a few minutes and then she turned to me. "Avery, right? It's great to finally meet you in person."

"You too," I said. She'd cut her hair and dyed it pink since we'd FaceTimed last year, but other than that, she looked pretty much the same. In her puffy lilac jacket with her new schnauzer, she looked much more what I'd thought Lucas's type would be before I met Ezra. No visible tattoos, anyway.

"My new best friend Frida and I have to head out," she said. "But I'll see you at work?" Lucas nodded. "Come over some time," she said to him and Ezra, and then she was gone.

Ezra nudged Lucas gently. "You want to go see the band?" he asked.

We all went over and watched the new band, set up on a makeshift stage in the grass. They did some sort of Brazilian folk music the small crowd seemed to love. We sat on the ground and Lucas leaned back against Ezra's chest. Ezra kissed the top of his head and Lucas tilted his head back for a real kiss. "You were right," he admitted. "This is nice."

"I'm always right."

We stayed for the band's set and headed back to the puppies for one last round of pats before we got back in the car. Lucas asked to see the pictures I took and I handed him the phone. He smiled at one and said to Ezra, "You do look very cute with the puppies."

Ezra took Lucas' hand. "Maybe in the future," he said.

At the house, Lucas went to use the bathroom (he was not, barring an emergency, using the park bathrooms, as he told us multiple times) and I pulled Ezra aside. "That was fun," I said. "I know you did it mostly for Lucas, but thanks for bringing me."

"I did it for both of you," he said. "Less stressed?" I nodded. "Good," he said. "Now let's get started on dinner."

*I*t's Valentine's Day and, to everyone's surprise, I spent it with Zehra! Well, everyone's surprise except Xio and Owen, who claim they totally saw it coming, but whatever. I'm too happy to care that they keep gloating.

A little bit of backstory. The Gayla was this weekend, and we were all super pumped for it. Zehra was stunning in a pale pink dress that went down past her feet and Xio and Owen got matching navy tuxes with pins over the breast pocket. Xio's were the asexual and nonbinary flags and Owen's were the gay and trans flags, for obvious reasons. Owen had been convinced it was going to be only us and the rest of Pride, even though we'd been selling tickets the last two weeks, so he was super relieved when we got there and there were a ton of students already in the gym.

I ended up borrowing my dress from Jess after I mentioned the event when she was over one night. She came for dinner with Frida and when I told her about the Gayla, she said she had an idea. Jess is shorter than me, but she's also curvier, so it ended up fitting me really well as a shorter dress. It's gold and flowy, but it's also shiny in a way that makes it rainbow in the right light. Perfect for a Gayla.

Jess laughed when I said this after she showed me a picture. "I've never really thought about that, but it is! Are you all donating the money anywhere?"

"The Trevor Project," I said, "and The Dominique Nolan Center."

"The Trevor Project sounds really familiar," Jess said. Frida nudged her hand and Jess passed her a piece of chicken.

"It's pretty famous," I said. "They deal with mental health for queer and trans teens. Suicide prevention. Things like that."

"That's amazing!"

"Yeah, we get a bunch of donations from the parents and everything too. We got a really big one from the university this year, which was super cool."

Jess looked over at Lucas and laughed. She stopped when he saw his face. Like a deer caught in headlights. "What?" I asked.

"Oh, just, we processed that donation," Jess said. "I didn't realize what it was for."

Anyway, I'm getting sidetracked. Back to the Gayla. Ms. Chang greeted us at the door by the gym. "You all look incredible!" she said. The five of us had come together: me, Xio, Zehra, Owen, and Owen's boyfriend, Connor.

"Thanks," Xio said, spinning a little so Ms. Chang could see the whole tux. Owen's parents waved at our group from the other side of the gym. They were chaperoning this year and had asked me a few weeks ago if Lucas and Ezra would be interested. I lied and said they were busy. I still feel weird about not having parents like everyone else, even though no one would have known they were with me except my friends.

Owen continued to gape at the crowd. "So many people came!" All of us laughed at him. Well, all of us except Zehra. She'd been quiet in the car and only smiled when she realized someone was watching her. Something was clearly wrong, but I didn't know what.

Pretty much everyone else from Pride was already there, so we all congratulated each other. Shawn, a sophomore, was the DJ and a couple juniors worked the food/refreshment table. I asked Zehra if she wanted to get a drink and she shrugged. "You go ahead," she said.

I sat next to her. "What's wrong?" I asked.

"Nothing's wrong."

"You know you can talk to me," I said. "Right?"

Zehra nodded and looked around. "I . . . Maybe we can get some air."

We left the gym together. A selfish part of me was hoping she was going to confess how much she liked me, but I knew something was much more wrong than that. We walked out front and Zehra sat on the ground against a pillar. I sat with her and she said, "I got a college letter today." She fidgeted with her fingers. "It was Hampshire."

I hugged my arms around myself, and not just because I'd left my jacket inside. "Oh." From her reaction, it couldn't be an acceptance.

She blinked back tears. "I haven't gotten any others," she said. "What if I don't get in anywhere?"

"That's ridiculous," I said. "Of course you'll get in somewhere." I tried to remember Ezra's words. "You're so smart and any school would be so lucky to have you, Zehra. Literally all of us are freaking out right now."

"I'm not that smart," she said.

"Are you kidding? You're the only person I know who can tell me every single move there is in Olympic figure skating. I didn't know what a cephalopod was until I met you. You always knew what to say this week when Owen was panicking about the Gayla and you saw that Devin was a jerk way before I did."

"Everyone knew Devin was a jerk," she said with a small smile.

"But you know so many other amazing things," I said. "You're amazing."

Zehra went super still. "Really?" she breathed.

"Really," I said. "Zehra —"

"Can I kiss you?"

"I . . . What?"

Zehra blinked. I could barely breathe. She wanted to kiss me. She really wanted to kiss me. We stared at each other for a second and she said, "I'm so sorry, Avery, I don't know what I was thinking. Please forget I asked."

"No, I . . . Don't be sorry," I said. "I've wanted to kiss you for a while." My face heated up and I must have been bright red, like Lucas gets when girls try to flirt with him. Relatable. Lucky it was dark outside.

"Me too," she said quietly. She bit her lip.

My heart pounded. "You can kiss me," I said. "If you want." My brain whirred too fast for me to keep up.

She did kiss me then. It was so, so different than kissing Devin. It was slow and sweet and I felt like I could drown in that kiss and it hadn't even ended, but I already wanted more. She pulled away first.

Her lips were so damn soft, wow.

"Was that ok?" she asked. I nodded and she said, "Can I kiss you again?" I nodded again and we both leaned forward.

We stayed outside for a while, until Zehra realized Owen was probably going to give his speech soon. We walked back into the gym together, where Xio and Owen screamed at us for two very different reasons.

"Are you two really holding hands?" Xio screeched. "I've been waiting for this to happen!"

"Where the hell were you?" Owen seethed. "I have to give my speech in five minutes."

Zehra and I both laughed. "Owen," I said, "we're here. It's ok."

Owen rolled his eyes and stomped off, probably to vent to Connor. Xio pulled us to the side. "Did you guys kiss?"

Zehra laughed. I grinned to myself.

Owen got up on the raised platform with the DJ and stepped up to the microphone. Shawn cut the music and Owen said, "May I have everyone's attention please?" We all turned to him. Owen stayed calm even with dozens of eyes on him (couldn't be me) and continued, "I love y'all."

The crowd laughed. Zehra, Xio, and I grinned at each other. "No, really," Owen said, "it's so awesome to see you all here tonight. I was so worried it would be just me and like three other people. It's so easy to forget that there's so much love and support when you're trying to ignore the haters in the halls and not read the comments under the articles about the anti-trans bills online, but you all make me so freaking happy."

There were some cheers to this. They died down and Owen continued, "When I first came out as queer and trans, my parents were super supportive, but they were also worried. They know it's hard to be the things that I am, but they didn't realize being part of the LGBTQIA umbrella means you get this super awesome community. My friends are awesome, y'all. Shout out to all of Pride, but especially my girl, Zehra, and my theydies, Xio and Avery." He waved over at us and I blinked back sudden tears. I forget sometimes how lucky I am to have these guys.

"Shout out also to Ms. Chang, who makes this happen every

year." There was brief applause and Xio whistled. Ms. Chang, who was standing on the side of the stage, waved a hand in dismissal, but she was smiling. "Basically," Owen said, "we're going to party all night in celebration of us and all the money we raised in ticket sales, half of which is going to The Trevor Project and the other half of which is going to The Dominique Nolan Center in DC."

The applause started again and Connor joined Owen on stage. They kissed quickly and the applause went up to eleven and Shawn started the music again as Owen and Connor left the stage holding hands. It was the best.

Compared to all that, actual Valentine's Day was pretty uneventful. Zehra and I went skating after school and then got dinner at Pulcinella's, which is a new Italian place downtown. It wasn't fancy like the place I went with Devin, but it was great in a different way. I felt more like myself. We still dressed fancy, in nice dresses and heels, and Zehra's mom let us borrow her car because she's the best.

The one terrible thing happened when I got home. The door was unlocked, which I knew meant Lucas and Ezra were home. Lucas is too anal to leave the door unlocked while no one is there.

They were definitely home. I threw the light on and screamed. Lucas and Ezra were on the couch, or Ezra was on the couch and Lucas was on Ezra, actually attached at the face. I caught a glimpse of Ezra's hand up Lucas's shirt before Lucas yelped and fell over.

He sat up quickly. His face was scarlet. "Avery." He cleared his throat. "I thought you were going to text me when you were on your way home."

"I did," I said a little too loudly. "Maybe you missed it while you were busy humping your boyfriend on the couch." At least they were wearing clothes. My God.

Ezra coughed quietly. Lucas somehow turned redder. "Yes. Well. Er. How was Zehra?"

Only Lucas would try to have a conversation right now. "I'm going to bed." I stormed out of the room and shut my door behind me. They could have at least locked the door. I heard them walking down the hall and shuddered. I would never be able to scrub my brain of what I'd just witnessed.

I checked my phone quickly before writing this. I opened a text from Zehra and wrote her back:

Zehra:
I had a great time tonight! :)

Me:
me too. i really like hanging out with you

I smiled to myself and held my phone to my chest. Being with Zehra is so easy in a way that being with Devin never was. I don't know how else to describe it. It's like I'm me when I'm with her, but amplified to the point where I'm finally comfortable in my own skin.

Zehra is the coolest girlfriend. She brought me some flowers from her mom's garden yesterday because, "They made me think of you," which, swooning right now. Xio laughed at us, but they told me later that they thought it was sweet, too. "I've never seen her be so romantic," they said.

Xio and I were at their house because they're babysitting/catsitting while their parents are away this weekend. We were pretending to do homework at the kitchen table while seven-year-old Elise watched cartoons in the living room.

"I feel like I need to do something for her now."

Xio shrugged. "Gift giving is Zehra's love language. She always gets me and Owen little things for our birthdays, but she doesn't seem to mind when we forget to do the same."

Gift giving was definitely not my love language. Quality time, maybe? Not physical touch. Honestly, for the best. Even though Zehra doesn't mind being touched, she's definitely not "touchy."

"Don't overthink it," Xio said. They peered around the doorway and added, "I think Ellie's asleep on the couch. She's only this quiet when she's sleeping."

"I can't imagine having a sibling so young." On the other hand, that was me and Lucas, just the other way around.

"I love it," Xio said. "I'm basically a fun aunt and sibling all in one." They peered around the corner again. "I'll miss her so much next year."

"You're not going far, though." We hadn't heard back, but all of Xio's schools were close, plus they were like ninety eight percent sure they were going to Millboro already. They'd get a big discount because of their mom. So would I, actually, because of Lucas, but Millboro didn't have a big art program.

"It'll still be so different not living with her. I can't believe she's seven already."

I nodded and flipped a page in my social studies textbook. Xio isn't Lucas and Xio's relationship with their sister isn't my relationship with my brother, but it was still a little déjà vu-y to talk about. I wondered if Lucas ever missed me after he went away. I wondered if Xio would ever say any of this to Elise when they left or if Elise knew how important she was to Xio. I hoped she did.

Lucas picked me up from Xio's for dinner and we got takeout on the way back, since Xio lives on the other side of downtown. "They're always welcome to come to our place," Lucas said as we pulled into the driveway.

"Sure," I said. "Thanks." My friends all know about Lucas and Ezra and my whole living situation, but I still felt kind of private about it. Xio had only come over the one time to help me get ready for my date with Devin. Maybe I'd start with introducing them to Zehra.

As soon as we got home and Lucas locked the door behind him, there was this loud BANG! from the kitchen. "Ezra?" Lucas hurried down the hall. I went after him but froze in the doorway. One of the glass plates had shattered. Splintered shards littered the floor. Glass crunched under Lucas's shoes as he ran to examine Ezra's bleeding hand. "What happened?"

"Plate slipped while I was putting the dishes away. I'll clean it."

Lucas held out an arm before Ezra could take a step. "Love, you're not wearing shoes."

Ezra looked down at his bare feet. "Oh."

To me, Lucas said, "Could you get the first aid kit in the bathroom? Our bathroom. Under the sink."

I nodded and went. I'd only been in Lucas and Ezra's room once before, the day I moved in and Lucas showed me around. It was carpeted like my room, with a queen-sized bed dead center. All of the furniture was matching dark wood, from the dresser to the bookshelves to the bed frame. The bookshelf was full to bursting, with books by authors like Rafael Frumkin, Sara Nović, and Racquel Marie.

Photos of Lucas and Ezra littered every available surface, plus the walls. Familiar faces appeared in some of them. They had one photo of the two of them and Jess at the park, Jess and Ezra wearing matching aviators, and one of Lucas and Daphne from years ago, both wearing sweatshirts from the colleges that would become their alma maters. I realized with a jolt that they had one of me and Lucas on the wall next to the window, from Lucas's high school graduation. Nine or ten-year-old me beamed at the camera, tucked under eighteen-year-old Lucas's arm. I had no idea then how strained our relationship would become.

By the time I got back to the kitchen, Lucas and Ezra had

somehow navigated the glass shards on the floor and were sitting at the kitchen table. Lucas took the kit from me and said, "Can you sweep the glass?"

"I'm not your maid, Lucas."

"I know." He took a pair of silver tweezers out of the kit. "I'm asking if you wouldn't mind." He leaned forward and began prying a sliver of glass from Ezra's palm, so it was either watch this nauseating mini-surgery or sweep. I went to get the broom from the closet in the hall.

"What happened?" Lucas asked Ezra as I came back in.

I turned so I could see them. Lucas focused on prying splinters from Ezra's skin, eyes narrowed in concentration. Ezra was watching Lucas work on his hands with entirely too much fascination. "The plate fell," he said again.

Lucas put the tweezers down (thank God) and reached for the disinfectant. "Sometimes," he said slowly, "when you're very angry or upset, you have a tendency to shove things into place or break something by accident." He was so calm, so unlike my brother I had to wonder if he hadn't been replaced by some sort of clone. "Correct me if I'm wrong," he continued, "but something very similar happened with a wine glass the night your step-dad died."

A shadow passed over Ezra's face. "No one died," he murmured. Lucas said nothing, just reached for the Band-Aids, but we all knew he was listening. "It doesn't matter," Ezra said. "It's not important." He sounded like me when I was telling him about Zehra and Devin and everything. It was a little unnerving.

"Does it have anything to do with seeing your doctor today?"

I didn't know Ezra had gone to the doctor. Ezra's lips twitched into a deep frown. "My inflammation numbers are up," he said. "It's just frustrating." I guessed the inflammation numbers had something to do with how bad his arthritis is. Actually, now that I looked at him properly, his clothes hung a little too loosely off his already thin frame. His eyes had dark circles under them.

"Frustrating," Lucas said, "and not at all unimportant." He put the Band-Aids away and clasped Ezra's newly bandaged hands in his. "I'm sorry."

It took me a minute to realize Ezra had tears in his eyes. "I'm so tired, Lucas." His voice wavered and he blinked rapidly.

"I know. You're allowed to be."

"Yeah." He freed a hand and wiped a stray tear. "Sorry."

"Don't apologize." Lucas took Ezra's hand back and kissed the back of it, bandages and all. It was so tender, so intimate that I had to look away.

"They're emailing the insurance company again. Like that will make a difference."

"It might," Lucas said. "In the meantime, Avery and I are both here for you. Right, Avery?"

Both of them looked at me, Lucas expectantly and Ezra a little startled, like he'd forgotten I was there. "Sure," I said, mentally kicking myself for not having anything more reassuring.

Ezra glanced at his and Lucas's intertwined hands. "I'll replace the plate."

"I don't give a damn about the plate," Lucas said. "We can get one at the dollar store for a couple cents."

"You won't," Ezra said with a faint smile. "You need them to match."

Lucas laughed and Ezra's shoulders relaxed just a little. Ezra looked back at me. "I can finish that," he said, gesturing to the broom in my hands.

I shook my head. "I'm almost done," I said. I swept the last of the glass shards into the dustpan and tossed it all in the trash.

"We did pick up takeout," Lucas said. "If you're hungry." Ezra nodded and Lucas went to get the bag where we'd dumped it in the doorway.

I fidgeted with the broom. Ezra looked down at the now clean floor. "Sorry you had to clean up my mess," he said softly. He was especially pale, too. I hoped that was just the florescent kitchen lighting.

I wish I told him it was alright. I wish I told him what I realized later — that it meant a lot to be to see him cry and break down and be human. I wish I said something about how odd it was to see Lucas so calm when Ezra was so rattled, like they had some sort of personality transplant. Instead I said, "I don't mind," and then Lucas was back with the bag of lukewarm Chinese food. He kissed Ezra's cheek and asked me to grab silverware.

That night, I went to use the bathroom before bed and heard Ezra crying down the hall again. Like, violent sobs, couldn't get words out crying. I stood outside the bathroom in the dark and listened to Lucas's muffled voice on the other side of the bedroom door, probably reassuring Ezra and telling him it was ok or something, and the petty part of me wished for one more thing. I wished Lucas could read me like he could read Ezra, that maybe then we'd know what to say to each other.

From: admissions@artinstitutechicago.edu
To: avery.marsh@gmail.com
Subject: Congratulations

Dear Avery,

Congratulations! It is an honor and a pleasure to inform you of your acceptance to The School of the Art Institute in Chicago. We at SAIC were very impressed by your portfolio, especially your work with acrylics, as well as your Common App essay. We believe you would be a valuable asset to our institution. Attached is everything you should need to get you started, including a map of the campus, a list of our majors and their

requirements, and your scholarship package, among other things.
Feel free to reach out to us with any questions. We look forward to seeing you on campus come August.
Sincerely,
Alexis de la Vega
Admissions Counselor

I'm going to college! I'm officially in at The School of the Art Institute in Chicago! I still have six other schools I'm waiting to hear back from. Purchase was a rejection, which I would be freaking out about if I wasn't already in somewhere. The next six could be rejections for all I care. I'm going to college! Plus, they gave me scholarship money! I haven't actually spoken to Mom about the finance part of it. She hasn't helped me with any of the applications or anything and I haven't even told her about Chicago. Maybe I should text her.

Zehra also got an acceptance this week, so we've all been celebrating. I know this isn't the most important part, but it's great to be dating someone my friends actually like. According to Xio, Zehra's had a crush on me since like week three and I and I keep thinking of how amazing it would have been if we'd gotten together sooner. No Devin, no weirdness between me and my friends. I knew she was funny and sweet and just the best, but somehow I didn't see her like that until way later. We figured it out though, so I'm trying not to beat myself up about it too much.

It's fun to hang out with our friends and not have to hide any part of ourselves. Like last weekend, we went up to the roof of the school (the first time they took me to do that back in October I freaked out the whole time) and smoked and it was just really nice to have Zehra curled up next to me and my friends be excited for us. Xio took a photo with their Polaroid of me and Zehra with my head on her shoulder and I put it up on the cork board in my room, under the photo of the four of us Connor took at the Gayla. Lucas saw the new photo and asked where we were when we took it, so I just said school. I'm not going to tell him we were getting high on the roof. Spare me.

Speaking of Lucas. I've met Zehra's parents dozens of times and they're super nice to me even now that I'm dating their daughter. Zehra, though, hadn't met Lucas and Ezra except in passing, so I finally invited her over for dinner one night and probably drove Lucas up the wall the whole week before. "Try not to be a total dork," I said one evening three days before they met. Lucas was reading on the couch.

"I won't." He didn't even look up from his book. It was a poetry book by Danez Smith, which he's read about a million times before. His copy is so worn that a few of the pages are falling out and the balloon on the cover is faded from Lucas touching it too many times. At least his taste in books is better than his taste in movies.

"Really, Lucas."

"I won't scare your girlfriend away," he said. He still didn't look up from the book. I'm so done with him.

The actual dinner went well though. Lucas made like three

dad jokes too many, but Zehra liked him anyway because she somehow doesn't think he's as big a dork as I do. She agrees with me that Ezra is really cool because duh, of course he is. "They're both cool," Zehra insisted after. She'd driven her mom's car and I walked her to it outside. Then we were just standing there. Neither of us wanted to say goodbye yet.

I rolled my eyes. "Lucas is a prat."

"He loves you," Zehra said. "It's obvious."

"He has to love me," I said. "He's my brother." Zehra opened her mouth to respond, but I cut her off. I wasn't in the mood to rehash all my annoying family drama. "I'll see you Monday?" I asked. Zehra nodded and kissed me quick.

Inside, Ezra winked at me. "She seems really great, Avery." I grinned way too wide and Ezra laughed.

It's great that Zehra and I can share our lives with each other. Devin never introduced me to his parents and I never felt close with any of his friends. I know I keep comparing them, but Devin was my first real relationship before Zehra and it's all so different.

Zehra actually respects me, for one thing. She's not a virgin and I think it matters less to her, but she said we can take our time. It's not like I don't want to have sex, but I don't want to regret it later. I would have regretted losing my V-card to Devin for sure. I don't think I'd regret it with Zehra, but I don't want to rush, either. It was definitely strange to ask, especially because of everything that happened with Devin, but she was super understanding. "We won't do it until you're ready," she told me.

Anyway, I'm not with Zehra tonight because Lucas promised to take me out for my first college acceptance, but obviously there's a reason I ended up spending most of the night in my room writing this instead of at said dinner or with my girlfriend. Lucas called me at a quarter till six. "I'm so sorry," he said, "something came up at work. Do you think we can celebrate next week?"

"Sure," I said, even though it sucked. I mean, if he told me earlier, I could have made other plans, but whatever.

"Thanks Avery," he said. "I'll be home late." Then he hung up and I had nothing to do but my homework, which I obviously wasn't going to do until later.

I came out of my room later to see what we had for dinner, since Lucas was working and Ezra was sleeping off an injection. The drugs he's on now make him tired and they barely help with the pain. He always says he's fine, but then he ends up falling asleep at the table or on the couch. That, and he had some pain and a headache from the fibro earlier, so he just wasn't in the mood to do anything. I made some dairy-free Annie's for nostalgia reasons and ate by myself and came back to my room to actually start on my homework.

The door opened when Lucas got home and he crept quietly down the hall, probably because he knew Ezra was exhausted. He stopped outside my door there and hovered for a moment. He had to know I was in there, since my light was on, but after a moment he walked past and went to his own room without even saying hello.

I woke up yesterday to a text from Owen.

Owen:
Devin the trashcan broke up with his girlfriend!!!

Xio:
Lol he deserves it

Zehra:
How do u even kno this?

Owen:
Lol ex-gf is in band with me she just posted
about it

Xio:
Good for her imo!

WHEN I DIDN'T ANSWER, Zehra texted me separately.

Zehra:
U ok?

Me:

ofc! just getting ready for the bus

I added a heart, hit send and put my phone away. I tried not to think about it, but that's exactly what I did all day. It wasn't about me wanting to be with Devin at all. I just kept thinking about what happened, and that made me wonder if the new girlfriend had to go through the same thing. It's not like I could have reported Devin either way, since he didn't actually hurt me, but I can't help feeling guilty thinking about if he took it out on her or did to her what he did to me. Zehra kept shooting me looks, but she didn't say anything.

Lucas must have noticed something was off at dinner, or at least he acted weird about it. He kept starting to say something then stopping. I came back to my room after that and didn't do my homework and tried to go to sleep early and failed. Around one in the morning, I got up and went to the kitchen to grab a glass of water and ran into Ezra, who was at the sink doing the same thing. He raised his eyebrows at me. "What are you doing up?"

"Couldn't sleep," I said. "What about you?"

"Same," Ezra said. He shuffled slowly over to the table with his glass.

I grabbed my own and went to fill it. "Pain?" Ezra jerked his head in a way I knew meant yes without him saying yes. I sat diagonal from him and asked, "Is it the arthritis or fibro?"

He sipped his water. "Fibro. For tonight at least." It was easy to forget Ezra was so sick all the time when he was taking me and Lucas to the park to pet puppies or talking to me about my crush on Zehra or college apps. It's sad to think about, especially considering he tries to keep that happy mask on all the time.

"Is that because of the numbers? The thing you were talking about after you saw your doctor?"

Ezra hesitated. "I shouldn't have said anything. It doesn't matter." See? Sad. It was totally reasonable to be upset that his body hated him.

"You didn't," I said. "You just broke a plate." I didn't tell him I heard him crying again later. It didn't seem like the time.

Ezra cracked a small smile. "No, the fibro isn't affected by my SED rate."

"What does it feel like?" I asked. I'd read a bit on the internet, but everyone said fibro was different for different people and hard to describe in general, which makes it wildly difficult to diagnose. There are no tests for it or anything. I asked Ezra about it when I first looked it up and he said he'd had to diagnose himself and tell his doctor about his research before she would consider it.

Ezra frowned, a slight movement in the dark, thinking over his answer. He drank again. At last he said, "Arthritis is like something is stuck in my joints. Something that's too big to be in there and then I can't bend them the right way without pain. It feels like burning when I do. It messes with my stomach, too, and then it's hard to eat. The fibro is . . . heavy. Heavy and like my bones have knives and they're trying to . . . to stab their way out of my skin."

Was he kidding? How does a person function like that? "All the time?" I asked, a little breathless.

"Not like that all the time," he said quickly. "Sometimes it's less or sometimes I don't feel it at all." He shrugged. "Tonight's not great though. The cream wasn't really working, but I ate a weed cookie a little bit ago. And no, I won't tell you where I keep them."

Actually, I found his stash a while ago, but I wasn't about to eat one when I knew they were for Ezra's pain. "Nothing stops it completely?"

He made a face. "My doctor prescribed me something once," he said. "It made me . . . numb. I couldn't move well. I don't know how to describe it. It targets nerve pain, so it made sense. It was just a little scary."

"Oh my God." A *little* scary? That was absolutely horrifying.

"I'll be fine," Ezra assured me. "I shouldn't be telling you this."

"I'm not a kid, Ezra. I hate that everyone keeps treating me like a kid."

"You technically *are* a kid."

"I'm seventeen. You guys can trust me with things. I'm not five."

Ezra studied my face for a moment. His bright eyes shown in the darkness. "You're right," he said. "You're right. That's not fair to you. It's not you, Avery. I never . . . It's hard for me to admit I need help sometimes, ok? But it's not you." He traced the edge of the glass.

"Why won't insurance pay for the new meds?" I asked. "For the arthritis?" I brought my knees up to my chest.

"They're more expensive than what I'm on now," Ezra said. "They want to exhaust all treatment options before they fork over the money. Which includes me being on this drug for almost a year already." He sipped his water and set it down slowly. An inexplicable smile tugged at his lips. "Lucas offered to marry me so I could switch to his insurance."

My feet slipped and hit the cool wooden floor. I almost choked on my own drink. "I'm sorry, what? When?"

"A few months ago. Before Christmas."

"He *proposed*?"

"Relax," Ezra said. "We're not getting married any time soon."

"So you said no."

"It wasn't exactly a dream proposal. I know marriage is just a formality, but I don't know. Is it so bad I want to marry Lucas because I love him and not because I have old person joints?"

It was a stab at humor, and a rhetorical stab at that, but part of me felt like he was really asking. It must suck to think he didn't deserve the fairytale. "I don't think so," I said.

Ezra shrugged. "What's keeping you up?" he asked.

"It's not important." It wasn't little pain knives trying to rip their way out of me or a non-proposal proposal.

He arched an eyebrow. "You don't have to tell me," he said, "but I'm here to listen. Lucas is, too."

I legitimately snorted. I couldn't help it. "Lucas doesn't care."

Ezra didn't say anything for a minute. I was afraid to look at him. I get that he's in love or whatever, but did he not realize Lucas kept bailing on me? At last, Ezra said, "Lucas felt really bad about canceling that night, you know?"

I caught myself before my face fell and tried to play it off like I didn't care. I crossed my arms. "Whatever."

"Did he tell you why he couldn't make it?" I shook my head and Ezra continued, "His coworker had to leave early after her kid got suspended. He was covering for her."

I frowned. "Why wouldn't he tell me that?" I might have understood better if he'd had an actual reason for bailing on me and didn't just make me feel like he hadn't wanted to be with me.

"Lucas is . . . He doesn't want to make excuses for himself. I think he blames himself for not being able to do both."

"That's ridiculous," I said. He could've told me, even if he'd said something the next day. Like, hey Avery, sorry my coworker needed to bail, but I still give a crap about you and you getting into colleges is pretty incredible.

"It is," Ezra said with a small smile. "He cares a lot about you, and I know you care a lot about him." I was about to argue when Ezra held up a hand. "I know you pretend like you don't, but it wouldn't bother you so much if you didn't care, right?"

I shifted in my seat. "You guys are a weird couple, you know? You're always arguing."

"We challenge each other. I'd like to think we make each other better."

"I think you make him better," I muttered. Truly, there was not a single argument I'd overheard where I agreed with Lucas. Not about accessibility on campus, not about scholarships. I only agreed with him when he said Ezra needed to talk to his doctor more than he did, but that was ultimately Ezra's choice.

"Both of us," Ezra insisted. "He's changed my mind once or twice. I used to be very adamant that everyone who can come out should come out. He made me realize it's not that easy."

"He changed your mind once or twice," I repeated. "You guys argue like a hundred times a day."

"Yeah, well, we're both stubborn."

"It just sucks," I said. "I know he has to work, but he can't even check in with me after? He literally walked by my room and saw the light was on. He could've come in."

"If he had, would you have kicked him out?" I bit my lip and Ezra said, "He's terrified of rejection, you know." He turned away and said, "That's part of why he hasn't come out to your mom."

"She's not going to reject him," I said. "Just dismiss him. Make him feel like he's crazy."

"Much better, yes."

I tried and failed to suppress a small smile. "Yeah, I know."

"Do you want me to talk to him?"

I shook my head. "I just wish there was someone in my family who got it. I'm so sick of having to ask my parents to respect me." Maybe because it was late, or maybe because I'm a mess, tears welled up in my eyes. I blinked a few times but they didn't go away. I hoped Ezra couldn't see them with the lights off.

"That's really hard," Ezra said. "I'm not going to pretend to know what it's like."

I sniffed and tried to wipe my eyes discreetly with my sleeve. I know I did a bad job, but Ezra pretended not to notice. "When I first changed my pronouns, Mom told me I shouldn't tell anyone. She said I'd get over it and then I'd be embarrassed."

Ezra made a noise like an angry cat. "If it were up to me, I would've said something to her over the holidays."

"It sucks, but it could be worse. She didn't disown me or anything."

"It's not a contest, Avery."

"Do you think your mom would have been ok with it?" I asked him. "If you'd gotten to come out to her?"

"I'd like to think so. My aunt came out to her before she died and she was supportive. My step-dad's sister."

"That's good," I said. "What was she like? Your mom, I mean."

Ezra took a moment to think again. He took another drink. "She was . . . sad a lot of the time. But when she wasn't, she was really funny. She was sarcastic and I think a lot of people didn't get her sense of humor, but I did. She could always make me laugh."

"She sounds awesome," I said, both because it seemed like the right thing to say and because she really did.

"She was," Ezra agreed. "Look, take it or leave it, but know that with Lucas, he just wants to know you want to be around him. He's scared to make the first move." He drained his glass and rubbed his eyes. "The drugs are working, I think. I'm going to try and get some sleep. You should do the same, ok?" I nodded and he left. I went back to my room.

I fell asleep quickly after that but woke up exhausted at seven this morning. Ezra was still asleep when I woke up, but Lucas was sitting at the table. I grabbed some Frosted Flakes from the cabinet and sat with him. "Are you ok?" he asked. "You look tired."

I bit back a retort, something like "Thanks for the compliment" or "You look worse," and said, "Do you think we could still do dinner together? Ezra can come, too."

Lucas looked shocked. You'd think I'd just told the guy I'd adopted a fleet of puppies without telling him. "Yeah," Lucas said. "I'd really love to."

Ezra, he's a smart guy. Plus, he's the resident Lucas expert. "Ok," I said with a small smile. "Well. Just let me know."

I feel so bad. Zehra had been extra quiet starting maybe two weeks ago, like even when it was just the two of us. I asked her what was wrong last week, when we were alone on the roof together. It was Lucas and Ezra's anniversary, so I had to be out of the house because they were all over each other already like the full week before and I didn't want to be around that. Apparently, Ezra was sick last year on the actual date – no surprise – and made it up to Lucas with some sort of romantic outing. I asked Lucas to skip the details. This is the first year they're celebrating their anniversary on their anniversary.

Zehra and I had been taking a walk together by the school and we were passing the metal bars around the generator that act as a sort of ladder to the roof and I suggested we climb up. We sat for a while and I asked her, "Is everything ok? You've been acting different." Different wasn't the right word. Distant, maybe, or discontent, but since I'm not planning on being an English major, I didn't think of those at the time.

She shrugged. She shifted. Then she said, "Do you want to get back together with Devin?"

My stomach churned. I felt like I'd been slapped. "What? No. Why would you even think that?"

"It's just, last week, you were different after he broke up with his girlfriend."

Different again. Maybe she couldn't think of anything better either. "I didn't mean . . . I don't want to get back together with Devin."

"Are you sure?"

I nodded. "Yeah, Zehra, I really, really like you. I just felt awful when I heard." I told her that I'd been afraid he could've done the same thing to his most recent ex that he did to me, or maybe something worse. We've talked a little about what happened that night I went out with Devin for his birthday, but I told her more about how scared I was and how I feel sick every time I think about it, how Ezra's been helpful but I wished I could talk to Lucas about it. Zehra listened until I was done and I realized I was crying again. It seems like I'm always crying these days.

"I'm so sorry," she said. "I didn't know you were feeling that way."

"Oh, no, don't apologize to me." I brushed away the last of my tears and took her hand. "Maybe we can just tell each other when we're upset?"

Zehra laughed. I love her laugh. It's high and clear and beautiful. "Ok," she said. "Wow, yeah, we can just talk to each other." I laughed too.

I still feel bad about it, but this last week has been a lot better. Another popup festival happened in the park, so we all went for Zehra's birthday and they weren't doing puppies this time around, but they were hosting a ton of small businesses. We got tacos from a local food truck and sat on the benches by the playground, wiping the juices off our chins with fistfuls of napkins. After, we got ice cream from these older women who owned their own storefront downtown. I got oat-based chocolate chunk and Zehra got lemon sorbet and we switched halfway through like something out of a cheesy rom com.

The bands were all local and we watched a heavily pierced blues singer from the university for a while, until Xio complained they were cold. I live closest to the park, so we headed back there and found Lucas and Ezra in the kitchen covered in flour, handprints smeared into the white. They were standing just a little too close to each other and the flour was smudged in odd streaks around their lips.

At least they had the decency to look embarrassed I caught them making out for like the fourth time since I moved here. I know it's their house, but come on. Lucas cleared his throat and pulled at the collar of his formerly black, now flour-white T-shirt. "We're making bread if you all want some." Zehra suppressed a laugh next to me and fiddled with the charm bracelet I got her for her birthday.

"Since when do you bake?" I asked Lucas.

"He doesn't," Ezra quipped. "His job is to stand there and look pretty." Lucas scraped flour off the countertop and flicked it at Ezra. It landed in his hair and beard and aged him forty years.

"You guys are cute," Xio said with a grin. I rolled my eyes.

At any rate, all of us are going to college now! Xio already knows they're Millboro-bound which is amazing. Zehra and Owen are both still thinking about it, too, but with very different options. Zehra's schools are all tiny liberal arts colleges and Owen's are all the size of small cities. We got together this weekend at Zehra's to celebrate all of us leaving and her parents ordered us pizza (soy cheese for me and Owen, who's trying the vegan thing) and we made plans to visit Millboro next year, to see Xio and each other.

I'm a little scared. It was hard to leave my friends in California, but it's going to be even harder to leave these guys. This is the first time I've had a real queer community. This is the first time I've felt so seen. I talked to Zehra about this too, since we had our talk about talking, and she said she's scared too. About everyone, but also because high school relationships don't usually last. I know she's right, but I wish she weren't. Maybe because I already had to do the whole goodbye thing, it's hard to picture myself staying in touch long-distance, but I really want to try.

We finally did do a dinner with me and Ezra and Lucas last week, and Lucas promised we'd do something when I made a choice, too. I officially have six acceptances out of eight applications, with four of them offering enough money for me to realistically consider them. I did end up talking to Mom about it and she and Dad are going to pay the rest.

The schools themselves are The School of the Art Institute of Chicago, The Rhode Island School of Design, and The Pratt Institute and The New School, both in New York. I've never been to any of these places, so Lucas and Ezra are going to take me to them all in April and I'll make a decision by May. I'm excited for a new experience, if nothing else.

For dinner, we went to this new Japanese place Jess recommended and got sushi, which was pretty good. Lucas smiled and laughed and made jokes, but there were a couple times he thought no one was paying attention to him that he stared down at the table and frowned like something was seriously wrong. I don't know if something came up at work or what, but I didn't ask.

From: castillor@millborohs.com
To: lucaswilde@millboro.edu
Subject: Disciplinary Action

Dear Mr. Wilde,

Thank you once again for coming to meet me with such short notice. As we discussed, I found Avery, along with three of her friends, on the roof this weekend with a joint. As you know, the school roof is out of bounds and we do not allow substance abuse on campus.
As we also discussed, Avery's punishment will entail will entail a one-week suspension and four weeks of community service

after school at Millboro Meadows, the assisted living facility for the elderly. Her first day of service will be Monday, April 3.

Thank you again for your cooperation. If you have any questions, please feel free to reach out to myself, Vice Principal Crane, or my secretary, Mrs. Carlile.

Best,

Rodrick Castillo

He/him
Principal

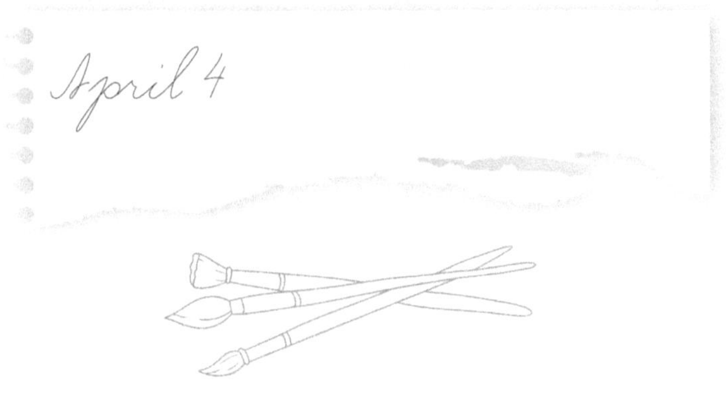

Never, ever in my life have I been in as much trouble at school as I'm in right now. Mr. Castillo, the principal himself, may or may not have caught us smoking on the roof this past weekend, so he called all the parents and Lucas. Quite frankly, it was embarrassing to have all these parents there and then my brother in his mid-twenties looking like a kid playing dress up in his dad's sweater. Actually, I'm not entirely sure that Lucas *doesn't* wear his dad's old sweaters.

Before all the parents got there, we were freaking out in the principal's office. Owen was convinced we were about to be expelled so then I started crying because what if they rescind our college offers and Zehra was trying to tell me her sisters used to get up to much worse crap at school, but anxiety makes logic difficult sometimes. Then the anxiety triggered my IBS and I ended up in the bathroom for ten minutes while the parents gathered outside. There's never a good time to have explosive diarrhea, but I feel like that had to be among the worst.

In the end, Mr. Castillo just yelled at us for a while and told us we'd have to do community service to make up for it. I felt bad for Xio because their mom is pretty strict and I knew they'd get yelled at even more once they got home, but I didn't anticipate Lucas going into full parent mode. When we got home and I went to go to my room, he said, "Not so fast, Avery."

I paused and turned. "I'm sorry?"

He put his bag down on the couch. "What the hell were you thinking, getting high on the school roof? Do you realize what could have happened?"

"God, Lucas, we've done it before. Don't act like an old man."

"That makes it so much worse," Lucas said. He ran his hands through his hair and made it stand up a little. "You're grounded. No social media for a week, no hanging out with your friends after community service."

I burst out laughing. "So now you're my dad? Screw you."

"You're living here, in my house –"

"I didn't want to! Do you think I'd rather be here with you in this tiny-ass town? I hate it here!" That wasn't true, but at that point I just wanted to hurt him.

"You're still grounded. I thought you were smarter than this."

Not gonna lie, that one hurt a little. "Fine. I hate you." I stormed off to my room and slammed the door shut and locked it and flopped down on my bed. I know I sounded like a little kid, but I was so damn angry I didn't know what else to say. What gave him the right to act like he cared now?

Lucas stomped after me. "Avery, we're not done." He knocked on the door. "Avery?" I didn't answer, so he tried to open it. "Avery, this isn't funny. Open the door." He knocked again. "Avery!" I rolled my eyes, put my AirPods in, and blasted Kendrick Lamar so I couldn't hear him anymore.

Maybe ten minutes later, the door swung open and I leapt off my bed. Ezra was crouched in front of the doorway with an unfolded paperclip in one hand. Lucas rushed past him and put a hand on my arm. "Are you ok?"

I threw him off. "What the hell? Yeah, I'm fine."

Lucas's eyebrows furrowed and he pressed his mouth into a thin line. "I thought you might've hurt yourself, Avery."

"Why would I do that? Jesus, Lucas. You pretending to give a crap for once isn't enough to make me suicidal."

Lucas flinched. "You can't speak to me like that." I think he meant it to be authoritative, but it came out soft.

"Enough," Ezra said. We both turned to him. "Avery, take out your headphones. We all need to talk."

"You could've knocked."

"We did," Ezra said. "You didn't hear us."

I glared at them both, but I did take the AirPods out. Ezra stuck the paperclip in his pocket and I gestured between him and the door. "How do you even know how to do that?"

"Don't worry about it," he said. Of course, now I want to know even more. Damn it.

I looked back at Lucas. "What do you want?" I asked.

Lucas opened his mouth to retort, but Ezra spoke first. "I think Lucas wants to apologize," he said.

The look on Lucas's face went from furious to astounded so fast it gave me whiplash. "You're making *me* apologize?"

Obviously, I thought, but then Ezra said, "Don't worry. Avery's next."

"I didn't do anything wrong," I said, even though that wasn't technically true.

"Both of you, shh. Now, Lucas, do you think maybe you were a little hard on Avery considering we were teenagers not that long ago?"

Lucas looked away. "I wasn't wrong." Cue internal eye roll here.

"Let's try that again."

Lucas sighed. He looked at me. "I'm sorry if I was hard on you. But –"

"No qualifiers. Are you sorry or not?"

"I'm sorry," Lucas said through clenched teeth.

"Why?"

Lucas sighed. "I'm sorry I yelled. And that I made you angry."

Ezra seemed satisfied, even though that was a terrible apology, and Lucas didn't even say sorry for calling me stupid. Ezra turned to me. "Is there anything you want to say to that, Avery?" I shrugged and toed the carpet. "Great, then do you think maybe you were out of line in the way you spoke to Lucas earlier?"

I kicked at the floor. "Maybe."

"So?"

I sighed. "I'm sorry. I don't actually hate you."

"Excellent," Ezra said. "Look, this is a new dynamic for everyone involved, so both of you need to talk to each other. Avery, it freaked Lucas out when you locked yourself in your room, alright? Can you try not to do that again?"

I should be perfectly allowed to lock myself in my own room, but I was done arguing. "Fine."

"I am sorry," Lucas said quietly. "I know I'm not your dad."

"Yeah," I said. "Whatever."

Lucas's brow went back to cartoonishly furrowed and Ezra put a hand on his chest. "I think we all need some space now. Avery, do you mind leaving the door unlocked?" I shook my head and Ezra said, "Great. Lucas, do you mind giving them some time now?"

Lucas threw up his hands and stalked out of the room, muttering to himself. Ezra shot me a wary smile. "He loves you. He's just as confused about this whole thing as you are."

I shrugged. "I'm not confused."

"Ok." We stared at each other for a beat longer before Ezra said, "If you need anything, I'm down the hall, ok?" I nodded and Ezra left.

That whole thing with Lucas was the worst part about all the smoking on the roof nonsense, since basically all we have to do is work at the old folks' home after school, which we already started and it's totally not a punishment, but none of us are going to tell Mr. Castillo that. Zehra and Xio are both good cooks, so they help out in the kitchen, and Owen and I help out with the cleaning.

We get to talk with the old people too and they have some cool stories. One of them, Miriam, used to be an artist and we talked about that today. She worked in pastels. Quite frankly, as long as I didn't say it was a punishment for illicit drug use, this would have looked great on college apps.

Lucas was already home when I got back tonight. He was in the kitchen, putting away dishes. He looked over at me and asked, "How was it?"

"Fine," I said. Easy. Fun.

"I am sorry," he said. "I . . . imagine it must suck to be yelled at by your brother-turned-guardian."

"Kind of."

"Ok. Well. I was going to order Chinese. Did you want your usual?" I nodded. Ezra left the room and I sat at the table with my school bag, alone. I sighed and got started on my homework.

$\mathcal{I}$'m still trying to make sense of everything that went down this last weekend, but maybe writing about it will help. Lucas, Ezra, and I left on Friday to look at The School of the Art Institute in Chicago, which was also a temporary break from community service with my friends where Miriam, the resident artist, and I spent last week talking about our favorite paintings. Really feeling that punishment.

Ezra promised he'd give us a native's tour of the city and show us all his favorite spots just like Lucas did for him in L.A., except that I'm actually invited this time. The night before my college tour, we stayed in adjoining rooms and Lucas bid me goodnight with, "Remember, breakfast closes at nine, so be ready by eight." I rolled my eyes. I did set my alarm, but the thought of doing a campus tour on an empty stomach was way more of a threat than an angry Lucas.

The morning of, I got up, took a quick shower, and threw on some clothes with three minutes to spare. I hopped on my phone and waited. I sent Zehra a "good morning :)" text and scrolled through TikTok and waited some more. Ten minutes passed with no sign of Lucas, who once lectured me for four weeks straight because I was fifteen minutes late to dinner in my own house. I grabbed my things and knocked on Lucas and Ezra's door. When no one answered, I pushed it open.

Lucas's eyes snapped up from his seat at the edge of the bed. His eyes fell on the clock. "Crap," he muttered. "I'm so sorry. I lost track of time."

The only light came from my own adjoining room and from the slats in the blinds. Ezra lay in a huddled mass next to Lucas. "Is everything ok?"

Ezra answered first. "Bad pain day," he said. "I'll be ok." His voice was hoarse and scary soft.

Lucas brushed Ezra's hair back from his eyes. "I'm not leaving you here," he said.

"I'll be fine," Ezra said. "You can't send Avery off alone." Lucas looked at me, then back at Ezra, and I realized with a jolt that was exactly what he wanted to do.

"If anything happens," Ezra continued, "I'll call you. It's just down the street."

I didn't say anything. Maybe it was selfish while Ezra was so sick, but I wanted my brother with me that day. All the other kids would have family there and I had no idea what to do on a college tour. "You promise you'll call right away?" Lucas asked.

"Promise," Ezra said. He closed his eyes. Lucas bit his lip and glanced at the clock again. In the end, he came with me, but the free scrambled eggs and bacon from the hotel breakfast bar didn't taste as good as I hoped knowing he nearly didn't.

The campus was pretty enough. It's in Grant Park, which is

Chicago's business district. Most of the classes take place in this one boxy, white building with all these galleries and art rooms. Maybe it's because I kept worrying about Ezra, but I didn't connect to it like I wanted. We got lunch in the cafeteria after the tour with two other students and their moms and the tour guide answered some of Lucas's distracted questions. Neither of the other students asked any questions either, so I didn't feel so out of place at least.

As soon as we finished lunch, Lucas grabbed my arm and whisked me back to the hotel. We rushed up the stairs, since the elevator was too slow for Lucas's liking, and back to our rooms on the third floor. It was still dark in Lucas and Ezra's room except for the cracks in the blinds and it took my eyes a second to adjust. The blankets were all bunched up on the other side of the bed. Lucas knelt by the bed and ran his fingers through Ezra's hair. "Hi, baby. How are you feeling?"

Ezra whimpered so quietly I almost missed it. He swallowed hard. "Hurts," he said.

"Did you use your cream?"

"I can't," he said. "I can't move." He shuddered and gripped Lucas's hand and Lucas brushed a tear from Ezra's cheek.

I didn't say anything, but I can't lie, I was freaking out a little bit. Lucas was surprisingly steady though. He didn't panic or threaten to call 911 like I thought he might. "If I get you your cream, can I help you with it?" Ezra nodded and Lucas said, "They have some tea downstairs you can drink, too. Can I get you some? I'll come right back."

Ezra made a noise Lucas must've taken as agreement and Lucas rose and headed for the door. To me, he said quietly, "Stay with him."

I nodded, but Lucas had already turned to leave. He shut the door behind him and I walked slowly over to the bed. "Was it bad last night, too?" I asked. Last night, we'd only had time to grab dinner and head back to the hotel, but Ezra did mention he hadn't been feeling great before we turned in. When Lucas asked him if anything was up, he'd said, "I'm tired," which is Ezra-speak for not feeling well.

His breath came out in shallow and erratic bursts. "Not this bad," Ezra said. "You don't have to stay."

Part of me was offended he thought he could get rid of me so easily. I sat at the edge of the bed instead. From here, I could see Ezra shaking. "What hurts?" I asked.

Ezra went quiet for so long I thought he might have fallen asleep. Then he took a sharp breath. "Everything," he said. "Everything hurts."

I was suddenly glad Ezra wasn't looking at me because I didn't think I could hide the sour twist of my lips or the tears threatening to spill down my cheeks. "I'm so sorry."

He whimpered again. "Talk to me," he gasped.

"About what?"

"Tell me about the tour."

I did. I told him about the campus, about the boxy, white building that was supposed to be pristine or whatever but felt more confining than anything else. I told him about the class-rooms I wanted to like and didn't because they were just too unfamiliar. I told him how we didn't spend that much time there, but by the time we left, I was more than ready. He was half-listening, but he probably did better than I would have if I were in that much pain.

The door swung open again and Lucas came back with the tea, effectively cutting off my rambling monologue. "They had your favorite," he said. He dug around in Ezra's bag and extracted small container and handed it to Ezra. Lucas slid an arm around him until he sat up completely. It took a while, since too much pressure from Lucas's arm sent shooting pains across Ezra's back. Lucas rubbed the cream on Ezra's skin as Ezra sipped slowly from the mug, wincing when he had to move. It smelled strongly of ginger.

After a while Lucas said, "How's your stomach? Have you eaten today?" Ezra shook his head. "Ok," Lucas said softly. "We can order something. What would you like?"

"Um. There's a diner around here, I think? They used to deliver." His voice shook and he tripped over his words.

"Let's order from there," Lucas said. So calm, like he was planning a picnic with friends instead of taking care of his scary sick boyfriend. Actually, scratch that, planning a picnic would totally freak him out. He'd worry about the weather and if there were any dietary restrictions and freak if anyone ran late.

We ordered diner food and I ran downstairs to get it. We spent the night at the hotel and Lucas let Ezra watch *Never Let Go* with Halle Berry on the TV even though he hid his eyes for the last half of the movie. Ezra lay with his head on Lucas's shoulder, still shaking a bit and taking sharp breaths when his pain shot up unexpectedly. Every time this happened, he squeezed Lucas' shand tightly and Lucas would run the fingers of his free hand gently through Ezra's hair.

In the morning, Lucas practically forced Ezra to take something for the pain, even though Ezra promised he was feeling better (than the day before, at least). After breakfast, Lucas and I did a quick tour of Chicago once Ezra reassured us for the millionth time that he wouldn't die while we were gone. We got to see The Bean, which everyone said we had to see and I didn't get the big deal? It's a silver structure that looks like an upside-down bean, hence the name, and apparently some guy owned the paint color at one point? I don't know. Lucas mentioned it briefly and I didn't care enough to ask. After that, we walked through some of downtown before we headed back to the hotel and called a Lyft.

The ride wasn't even ten minutes, but Ezra was pale and shaking again by the time we got to the airport. Lucas got a wheelchair from the airline people and demanded Ezra use it. "You're in pain," he said.

"I don't need it," Ezra insisted, but he was using my shoulder as a crutch and breathing funny again while Lucas held both their bags.

Lucas pinched the bridge of his nose. "Humor me, ok?"

He did, and he also fell asleep about five minutes after take-off, so it was just me and Lucas. Maybe fifteen minutes in, Lucas turned to me. "We didn't really get the chance to talk about the school."

As if I hadn't noticed. "It was fine," I said.

Lucas opened his mouth, closed it again, then said, "You know, I didn't love any of the schools I toured."

"Until Baltimore, you mean?"

"No. I mean I didn't dislike Baltimore and it was far from home, so I got on a plane and moved across the country."

I stared. "Ok, I'm sorry, that's ridiculous."

Lucas cocked his head in thought. "Maybe. But I don't regret my choices." He looked down at Ezra, whose head had fallen onto Lucas's shoulder once more, and gently brushed his hair back from his forehead.

"Sure." I mean, that's all well and good for him, but I'm hoping I'll like one of the other schools enough that I don't spend the next four years of my life at the least bad of four bad options. Besides that, I'm glad Lucas doesn't have any regrets, but would it be so bad if he regretted leaving me behind at least a little? I'm not a bad high school experience he can shake off.

We got back late and Ezra pretended like he wasn't in pain, but he basically winced with every step, so Lucas brought him to bed and I texted Zehra.

Me:
college hunting weekend was a bust

ill tell u all about it tomorrow

Zehra:
Sorry bb. Happy ur back tho!

I smiled at the phone. Down the hall, I could hear Lucas's muffled voice, but I tried to block it out. One person in my life would be happy to see me, at least.

It's official. I'll be spending the next four years of my life at (drum roll please) . . .

The Rhode Island School of Design!

We went the weekend after Chicago and stayed at a hotel in downtown Providence. Lucas and I both insisted that Ezra didn't have to come, but by Wednesday he promised he felt better (he looked less pale, at least) and wanted to go, so the three of us flew up together Friday after school. I didn't know anything about Providence or Rhode Island before I went, so I did some research at the hotel and found:

- Providence is the third largest city in New England, which surprised me.

- It was settled in 1636 by a Puritan theologian, which I also didn't know but I care about that a lot less.
- For the first time in my life, I will be somewhere that actually gets cold and stays cold in winter, though I could have figured that one out on my own.
- This city has one of the biggest queer communities in the northeast, which is my favorite fact.
- It has a surprisingly large theater scene.

Anyway, Providence was cool, but the school itself was amazing. The buildings are all super old, but that's much more my aesthetic than "big white block." There's this mansion that wouldn't look out of place in a horror movie – basically, it looks like someone took three buildings and stuck them together. The outside is white and pale brown and brick with a pale green roof and students hang out there at the cafe inside. The tour guide showed us their dorm, which is this limestone behemoth that also houses a library and cafe (so many cafes!). It's near Brown, so Providence is a pretty big college town.

I love it! I love it! I love it!

We went up to New York the next weekend because Lucas said we should still see the other two schools. Ezra's Aunt Andrea (technically his step-aunt, his step-dad's sister) met up with us for lunch and told us all kinds of embarrassing small Ezra stories. Like when he was six and he decided he didn't need to wear a bathing suit at the community pool. From my understanding, Ezra's step-dad was in his life from the time he was four or five, so he's close to that whole side of the family.

"You have to come visit more often," Andrea said after regaling us with a story about Ezra nearly drowning in the ocean at the age of eight because he refused to get out during a riptide. "And bring this one with you." She nodded at Lucas, who smiled down at the table.

"I will," Ezra said. "I'm almost positive Avery is about to move to Rhode Island, but we can always make a detour here."

"They're going to look seriously at all their options," Lucas insisted, even though Ezra was right.

I'd never actually been to New York before, so that was fun too. We didn't have time for a ton, but we saw Central Park, or part of it (it's massive!), and got hot dogs from a cart, which apparently you have to do in the city. There are food carts like every other block in Manhattan. It was really nice to spend the weekend back in a huge city, though after living in Millboro for almost a year, I don't know if I'd ever want to move back to L.A. full time.

We toured both schools on Sunday. We did the New School first and Ezra made it through that tour fine, but by the time we got to the Pratt Institute, his hip was swollen and he was limping.

"You don't have to come," I said. It's not like I didn't want him there, but he was leaning heavily to the left and his face was drawn.

"Are you sure?" he asked. I took it as a sign of how badly he felt that he didn't argue. I nodded and he said, "You'll tell me all about it, right?"

"I will," I promised. Lucas made Ezra swear he'd text when he got back to the hotel and call if he needed anything and then it was just the two of us again. We did the tour and talked to some students and then we met up with Ezra for dinner at a place called Green Symphony. He said he was fine after a few hours of rest and no walking and for once, Lucas chose not to argue with him.

Both schools were fine. If I had to pick between them, I'd probably pick Pratt, just because I'd rather live in Brooklyn than that part of Manhattan. It has a real campus too, which I didn't realize was important to me until I saw The New School, which is smack in the middle of a random street. I like the idea of being immersed in college, and while Pratt does have that, I knew I wanted Rhode Island before we left the admissions office.

Zehra officially chose Mount Holyoke this weekend and Owen is going to the University of Chapel Hill in North Carolina, so we're all in! We're all going to school! I can't believe it!

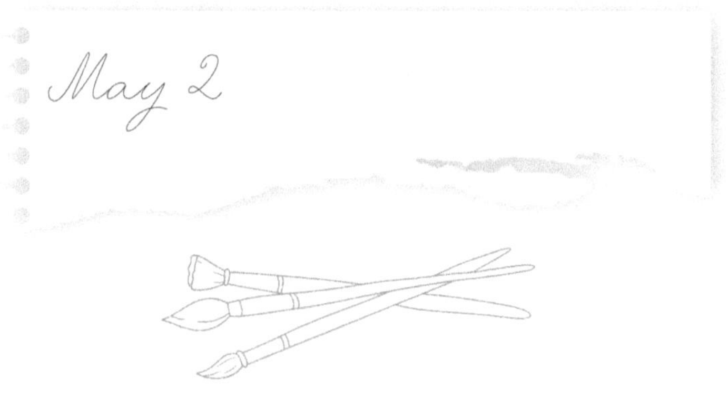

This last week has been absolutely wild. I feel like I say that every time I write, but it keeps being true. I guess that's what it's like to be officially college-bound!

First, I officially sent in my acceptance to Rhode Island! I made Zelma hit the actual "send" button because I was so nervous, but it's in! We did it! Lucas and Ezra are taking me out to celebrate this weekend and I am excited about it. They've both been super happy for me and even Lucas is being supportive. He brought up celebrating again without me saying anything.

I also finished my community service, but we're all planning on volunteering again over the summer. It would have been a great last day except that when we all got in Owen's car to drive home, after many faithful months of service, it refused to start. Owen's parents were both at work and Zehra's parents didn't pick up and Xio flat out refused to call their parents because they didn't want to get yelled at (fair), so of course I had to call Lucas to come get us. He was pretty chill about it, but then we had to do the whole "I'm glad you called" thing in front of my friends, which was totally embarrassing. Zehra thought it was "sweet" and basically all my friends love him. I don't get it.

Actually, that's a lie. Owen has said at least twice now that it's so cool my brother is gay and they all love having a queer couple they can look up to, which is valid, but I happen to know that if I'd never moved here, I'd still be living under the delusion that Lucas and Jess were dating. I'm glad my friends all like him, but it doesn't seem fair that they get Gay Icon Lucas Wilde when he was in the closet with me for so long.

Anyway, Owen's car is officially done for. RIP to the real one. Speaking of family — family meaning Lucas, not Owen's car — Mom sent me an email the other day asking if I wanted to come back for the summer. To California, to live with her. I'm so torn about it. I know that my and Zehra's time is limited and that my relationships with Xio and Owen are going to change once we all leave for undergrad, too, and I want to spend time with them. I also know if I don't go back to California, I probably won't see my parents again for a really long time.

I brought it up to Lucas and Ezra over dinner this week. Ezra listened and tried to offer some pros and cons and Lucas sulked and stabbed at his peas. I couldn't tell if he was annoyed I might stay or if he's annoyed I might go or if he's just annoyed in general. It bugs me that he doesn't even try to help. He acts all Dad trying to punish me for smoking pot, which Ezra takes all the time in cookie form and which will be legal for me in a little over a month anyway, but now that I could actually use advice it's like *he's* the child. Whatever.

Back to Zehra, though. The important part. We went out on

a date to celebrate both of us officially going to college next year. She borrowed her mom's car and we went to Pulcinella's, which has become a go-to place. Pulcinella's isn't uber fancy or anything, but she had her hair up in all these clips and she was wearing this flowery white blouse and her smile was stunning. She saw me looking when we got in the car after dinner and blushed. "What?"

"I think I want my first time to be with you," I said. It might have sounded random to her, but I'd been thinking about it a ton and even if we don't stay together forever or anything, I trust her. She's been there for me all year, even when I couldn't see how perfect we were together. She stuck with me through the Devin fiasco and she's just the best, ok? I wanted that connection with her.

Zehra couldn't stop a smile from creeping across her lips, but of course she didn't make it about herself because she's perfect. "Are you sure?"

I nodded. "How late are your parents going to be out tonight?" I asked.

Zehra checked her phone. "We have a few hours," she said. She was smiling wide now, and so was I. We got back to her place and basically, congratulations to me! I will no longer be going to college a virgin. Holy crap, I can't believe I'm saying that. I thought everything would be different after. I did feel different. More adult? Mostly though, everything was the same after. It was a little weird and scary, but Zehra kept asking me if I was ok and I wanted her to keep going. So scary, but in a good way? I couldn't figure out what to do with my hands and then Zehra's zipper got stuck, but we could laugh about it together and that made everything easier.

She made sure I was ok after and we cuddled in bed and it was really nice to just lay in her arms and hold her close. We kissed for a while and explored each other's bodies with our hands and whispered in the dark. She told me more about the first time she had sex, with a guy who graduated last year who was basically her Devin. He wasn't on the football team or anything, but he was older and he showered her with attention until he didn't, and then he pretended like he didn't know she existed when they saw each other in the halls. "That sucks," I said.

Zehra nodded. "I'm mostly over it," she said, "but I'm really glad I got to do this with you."

I leaned forward and kissed her gently. I have no idea how she keeps her lips so soft, but they feel so good on mine. She dropped me off after that and I opened the car door and she called my name like we were in a movie. I turned around and she kissed me softly. "I'm glad I got to be your first," she said.

"Me too," I said. I got out of the car with the biggest smile on my face and I couldn't quite rein it in when I got into the house, but I didn't care. I found Lucas and Ezra in the kitchen and asked about their night.

They looked at each other in that annoying way adults do, like you're not even in the room, and Lucas said, "It was fine. How was yours?"

"Good."

Lucas grinned. "Yeah?"

"Mmhmm. Goodnight!" I'm sure they know *something* happened. It's not like I was subtle and as annoying as Lucas is, he's also smart, but I don't care. I'm so happy I could die right now and I'd be ok with that. Not really, because I'm only seventeen and that would be tragic. I don't even know what I'm saying anymore. It's official.

I'm in love.

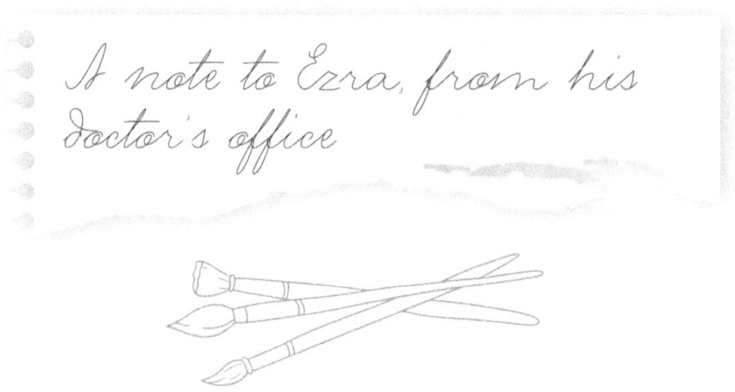

Hey Ezra,

So sorry for the delay. We were officially able to get the medication approval on file! Our infusion centers are limited in space due to "chair availability," so I had the team schedule you in an "urgent" slot which was 5/5. If you need to contact our infusion team for any reason, their number should be in your MyChart.

I did send this initial request for every 8-week dosing rather than 6 weeks. I didn't want the new plan to kick back with frequency issues and more work that would hold you up further. After your dose on 5/5, I will re-submit for every 6-

week dosing for you. That way, we have time to handle any insurance issues. Sound okay?

Let me know if you need anything else!

Nomi Chavez, RN

Nurse Coordinator
Millboro Hospitals Outpatient Specialty Clinics at East Village
Division of Rheumatology

If Mom still wants me to come back for the summer, I'd rather be anywhere but here. I know Mom doesn't give a damn about me either, but at least she doesn't pretend. There was no dinner to celebrate me going to Rhode Island in August and that would be fine because tonight was wildly terrifying and obviously I get that Lucas needed to be with Ezra. Like, I'm not the most terrible human on the planet, but is it so bad to want him to say, "I know you're probably scared, too, so do you want me to pick you up and we can be scared together?" It's like he doesn't think I have feelings or that I care about Ezra too. He barely even thinks of me as family.

Insurance finally approved the new meds for Ezra's IV infusion treatments and Ezra got his first one today. He's been off the old drugs for an extra week to prepare for getting on the new ones and he was feeling like actual garbage last night. Like his knee was swollen to the size of a large orange and his hip was bothering him, too, and he had a fever from it and then the arthritis triggered the fibro in his leg. Needless to say, he was really looking forward to getting the new treatment. He's had like fifty-eight billion injections since I got here and he's always a little tired and sometimes he gets those migraines, but mostly he's fine after them, so we assumed it would be more or less the same with the new stuff, but Lucas called me today around four freaking out because Ezra had a bad reaction to the new drugs. "He passed out," Lucas said. "He's in the hospital."

"Wait, what?" I paused an old episode of *Queer Eye* on the TV. It's Friday, so I was mostly planning on eating chips and being lazy until Lucas and Ezra got home and we all went out together.

"He hit his head," Lucas said. His voice cracked and he took a breath. "He hasn't woken up." A door slammed on Lucas's end.

"Is he going to be ok?" My own voice was high and scared and I hoped Lucas was too freaked out himself to notice. Ezra had to be ok. He couldn't not be ok.

"They didn't say much." Another door slammed and then a car started. "I'm going to the hospital now."

"Yeah, of course."

That's when it would have been great to hear "I'm so sorry" or "I'm on my way to get you first." Instead, Lucas said, "I have to go," and hung up the phone before I could answer.

I sat on the couch, frozen, not entirely trusting myself to do anything. I wasn't sure if I was upset or scared or mad or what, but whatever I felt was crushing me. Didn't he know I was terrified, too? Couldn't he have taken two seconds to say yeah, he had to cancel, but he was still proud of me? Ok, no, that's selfish. Oh God, was Ezra going to die?

That's when I picked up the phone.

Me:
are u guys still going out tonight?

Xio:
Yeah!! Are you coming?

Zehra:
What happened 2 dinner?

Owen:
I'm so ready to be drunk

Me:
dinner is cancelled

is the party still at diane's?

Xio:
Yeah but we're getting ready at Zehra's

I'll pick you up!

Diane lives down the street from Lucas and Ezra, but since we were getting ready at Zehra's, Xio came and got me around seven. We all did our makeup and tried on a couple outfits before we headed out. A girl who wasn't Diane greeted us all at the door and we went out back by the pool and I shared a beer with Owen and took a drag off of Xio's joint and danced and then there was another beer before Zehra took my arm. "Are you ok?"

"Fine," I said. I was a little tipsy, but not drunk enough to break down sobbing in front of half our grade.

"Do you want to walk with me?" I shrugged and she took my hand. We walked around front and sat on the front steps. A few stoners blew bubbles on the grass. "What's up?" Zehra said.

"Why would something be up?"

"You were supposed to go out with your family tonight," Zehra said. "Did something happen?"

Zehra was always self-conscious about not being able to pick up on social cues, but she was a little too perceptive about things like this. "It's just . . . Lucas," I said. "It's stupid."

"Bet it's not."

She reassured me the same way Ezra did. I wasn't sure if I wanted to laugh or cry. "Ezra got really sick today," I said. "He has arthritis and he got this new treatment but it made him sick. He's in the hospital and . . . It's stupid. And selfish. I just wish Lucas could've asked me if I wanted to come and wait with him or said he was sorry for canceling plans or something." I shrugged again. "I'm scared, too, and it's like he doesn't even care." Maybe I actually was drunk enough to break down crying, or maybe I felt like crying because my life recently is just one big, sad blur.

"You should tell him this," Zehra said.

"When?" I asked. "When his boyfriend gets home from the hospital? Next time he blows me off for work?"

"Yes."

I ignored her. I pulled out my phone and realized, to my horror, that the screen was black. "Crap," I said. "What time is it?"

Zehra pulled out her own phone. "Almost midnight."

I stood. "I have to go." I took off down the street before Zehra could stop me. She called my name, but I didn't look back. I pretended the tears stinging my eyes were from the wind. That's what I would have told someone if anyone asked, but they didn't. No one ever does.

Lucas's car was in the driveway when I got there, but not Ezra's. Ezra's car was probably back at the doctor's office or wherever the treatment happened. Still, that had to mean Ezra was home, right? Lucas never would have left him in the hospital. Oh God, please let Ezra be home.

I caught my breath out front and tried the door. It was open, which was a bad sign. I remembered locking it when I left, which meant Lucas was still awake. I opened the door as quietly as I could and slipped inside. Lucas was on the couch, his back to me, but he had to hear the door open. I hesitated in the foyer, then went into the living room and sat on the armchair. Better to get it done with.

"How's Ezra?"

Lucas wouldn't look at me. "He's home," he said quietly. "Sleeping."

"Good," I said. "Great." I tried not to look at how red his eyes were or the heavy bags underneath. I tucked my windswept hair behind my ear. He met my gaze and I realized he wasn't just mad. He was furious.

"It's past midnight. Where were you?"

"Zehra's," I said automatically.

"Don't lie to me. You smell like beer and weed."

I stood. "I'm going to bed." I should've come back later. I should've slept at Zehra's or something.

Lucas rose and came around the couch so we were standing face to face. "We need to talk about this."

"I don't need you to be my parent," I said. "I'm fine on my own."

"You can't just run off in the middle of the night," Lucas yelled. "I had no idea where you were. You weren't answering your phone and honestly, I had more important things to worry about tonight. You aren't a child."

That last comment had my blood boiling. He always acted like I was too young to know anything, and then that it was convenient for him, I was grown? "Only when it's better for you, you mean?"

"What's that supposed to mean? Avery, I was worried about you."

"No, you don't get to play the caring older brother," I yelled right back. "You made it clear you don't give a rat's ass when you moved to the other side of the country to get away from us."

Lucas took a step back. "I wasn't leaving you," he said. "I was leaving them."

"You still left." I was shrieking at this point but I couldn't seem to lower my voice. "You abandoned me, Lucas, and then all of a sudden Mom and Dad shipped me off to Nowheresville, Virginia, to live with a brother I haven't seen in years, who I don't know a damn thing about, who didn't say anything when I came out and I was getting absolute garbage from Mom and Dad even though he was living with his secret boyfriend this whole freaking time. But Mom and Dad don't care because they don't want me either and you pretend to give a crap until it's hard and then, forget it, but you know what? I don't care either. I'm done caring." I pushed past him so hard he fell against the couch, but I didn't stop. I came back to my room, the guest room, whatever, and finally burst into tears. If Lucas could hear me crying when he shuffled past my door minutes later, well, he didn't say anything.

It's four in the morning now and I'm so scared for Ezra and pissed off at Lucas and the rest of the world and let down for about the millionth time this year and I don't know what to do anymore. Maybe I'll call Mom tomorrow and see if she even still wants me to come back.

I woke up late this morning, almost noon. There were about eighty-five million missed calls on my phone from Lucas from the night before and worried texts from all my friends. I unplugged my phone and responded to Xio and Owen. I told them I wasn't feeling well, but I would be fine, then I texted Zehra.

Me:
im home safe! sorry for worrying u :(

Zehra:
Omg r u ok? What happened w Lucas?

Me:
i'm ok. i promise ill tell u everything later

things are just weird at home rn

but i do promise im fine

Zehra:
I'm just glad ur ok

I'm here if u need me!!!

I sent her a quick heart and set my phone aside. I'd have to tell her about going back to California eventually, but that seemed like an in-person sort of conversation.

I listened for any signs of life, but couldn't hear anything, so I threw on a T-shirt and jeans, brushed out my hair, and headed to the kitchen. Lucas sat at the table, facing the door. We made eye contact and I briefly considered running all the way back to California right then, but then Lucas gestured across the table. "Will you sit with me?"

The question caught me off guard. I crossed the room and sat slowly. "How's Ezra?" I asked. I knew it was mostly an anxiety thought, but I was half convinced he'd die in the night.

"Tired," Lucas said. "He's sleeping now, but we . . . talked this morning. He helped me realize some things." He took a breath. "Can we talk?"

"Aren't we already talking?"

"I guess so." He picked at the skin around his nail. Shifted a little in his chair. "Do you know much about my dad?"

I had no idea where this was going, but I decided to humor him. "I know he was sick."

Lucas started to say something, stopped, and then he said, "We were really close when I was little. I don't think he and Mom were a good match, necessarily, but maybe that's just in hindsight. He loved her. I know he loved her. Then he got sick . .

." Lucas trailed off and stared out the window. Birds twittered just outside.

After a minute he cleared his throat and continued, "Mom remarried and she had her new husband and I had no one. You have to understand, this was all in the span of a few months. I knew it wasn't Dad's fault. Of course it wasn't, but I was still so upset that he left me and Mom kept saying it was his fault for smoking and it was so much easier to be angry with him. Even when you came along, Avery, I loved you so much, but that house was going to kill me." He choked a little on the last word. I didn't know what to say. He reigned himself in and continued, "Do you remember when I was sixteen and I got so sick I had to go to the hospital for fluids?"

Before my ballet recital. "Yeah," I said quietly. A bad stomach bug, they said, but I suspected now there was more to the story. The house was warm, but my skin had broken out in goosebumps.

"I knew I was gay at that point and I tried to come out to Mom and she told me . . . She told me I'd get over it," Lucas said. "When I tried to push it, she yelled at me and told me I didn't know what I was talking about. She refused to talk about it for a week and whenever I tried to bring it up, she'd just start screaming. When your dad was there, he would just . . . watch her do it. I waited a week and told her she was right, that I was just confused, and it was such a weak excuse but she wanted me to be normal so badly she didn't question it."

The skin around his nail had begun to bleed, but Lucas didn't seem to notice. "No one else knew, Avery. I was so alone. That night I swiped a bunch of pills from the medicine cabinet. I couldn't take it anymore." Lucas sniffed and wiped at his eyes. "At the hospital, Mom . . . She yelled at me again. For doing that to her. When I came back, Mom and David wouldn't talk about it at all. They acted like it didn't even happen and I thought I was going crazy. I didn't know what to do except leave."

I couldn't breathe. I didn't know any of this. How could I have not known any of this? A piece of a conversation I had with Ezra about therapy came back to me. What had he said, exactly? *Lucas . . . would understand better than you think.* I thought he meant that Lucas would understand because *Ezra* had been in therapy. Not this. I never imagined this.

Another conversation rang in my head too. "Lucas, did you get the university to donate to The Trevor Project?" Jess mentioned they processed that donation, but she'd changed the subject so quickly and Lucas looked so freaked out by it. I hadn't even thought about it.

He nodded. "When you came out," he said, "I was so scared Mom would do the same thing to you. It sounds like she tried and you're just stronger than I ever was, but I also . . . There was always that fear. I wanted you to know how much you're supported." He shook his head. "I should have just told you. That's why I was so freaked out when you were locked in your room and I'm so, so sorry about that." It took me a second to realize what he was talking about. Last month, when we were yelling at each other about me getting in trouble at school and I locked myself in my room. Oh God, he thought I was going to hurt myself because that's exactly what happened to him . . .

He wiped his eyes again, but he couldn't stop the tears. "It wasn't fair for me to project all of that on you," he said. His voice shook, but he kept going. "I do think Mom loves me. I know she loves me. She loves both of us. I just don't think she knows how to love well. She's never known how to love well. The one person who saw me as worth anything left me alone and . . . and that's exactly what I did to you."

That was it. That was exactly how I felt. "Why didn't you say any of this?" I asked. I was crying now too, damn it.

"I should have," he said. "When Mom called me and asked me to take you, I was devastated. I thought, I can't believe this is happening again. I didn't realize it was already happening to you, that I made it happen." He was legitimately sobbing now. "I'm so sorry, Avery. I've been such a horrible brother and I wish I could change that, but I know I can't. Do you think you could let me make it up to you?"

God, I never wanted this. I wanted Lucas to understand, but I had never wanted him to hurt like this. Or maybe I had. I'd been so angry at him for not being the family I needed I forgot he was a freaking *person*.

"Yeah," I said. "Yeah, I can do that."

If anything, Lucas somehow started crying harder. I got up and walked around to his side of the table. He stood and pulled me into his arms and held me tight. I buried my head in his shoulder and Lucas whispered, "Thank you." He let me go and wiped his eyes again. "God, I'm a mess."

I shook my head. "You're not a mess," I said. "And you *are* strong."

His lips twitched up at the corners. "You sound like Ezra." He took another deep, slow breath. "Maybe we can reschedule your celebration for this weekend?"

"It's not about the freaking celebration, Lucas."

"I know," he said. "Can I give you one anyway?"

"Aw, so sweet." We both turned at the sound of Ezra's voice. He stood in the doorway, leaning heavily against the frame. A jagged, half-healed gash started just under his hairline and ended at the top of his eyebrow over a massive blue and purple bruise. His beard was fuller than normal after more than a day of not shaving. His T-shirt hung loosely around his torso and his eyes had dark circles under them to rival Lucas's, but he was smiling at us.

I ran and threw my arms around him. "You look like crap," I said into his shirt. "I'm so glad you're ok."

Ezra hugged me back and then I felt Lucas behind me. We stood like that for a minute, all of us huddled together, until Lucas said, "I came out to Mom this morning. Again."

Ezra took a step back and Lucas' arms slipped away. We stared at Lucas like he'd grown an extra head. "You did what?" Ezra asked.

"I called her after we talked this morning," Lucas said, gesturing between himself and Ezra. "I might've told her off on a few things. It came up while I was yelling at her for how she's treated Avery."

I couldn't believe he'd really done that. And for me? Damn it, Lucas, I was going to start sobbing again. "You're incredible," Ezra said. "How do you feel?"

A quick laugh escaped Lucas's lips. "Like I should be asking you that question." When Ezra urged him on, he said, "It's strange. It feels . . . I don't really know yet. I do know I hated having to hide how much I love you." Ezra kissed Lucas' cheek and I rolled my eyes. "Really though," Lucas said, "you were in the hospital last night with a concussion. You should be resting."

"I'll be on the couch," Ezra said. "I'm sick of our room."

"You've been awake in there for five minutes."

Ezra slid his arms around Lucas' waist. "If you watch a movie with me," he said, "I'll let you pick something that isn't horror."

Lucas laughed for real this time. "That might be the sexiest thing you've ever said to me."

"Ok, gross," I said. "I'll be making breakfast in here, so if you're going to make out on the couch, please do it quietly."

"We should all eat something," Lucas said with a pointed look at Ezra. To me he said, "And we'd be honored if you'd join us for a non-horror movie after."

"You're a dork," I said, but I was kind of touched. Lucas made us blueberry pancakes, even though it was almost one o'clock by then, and we ate them in front of the TV despite Lucas's usual insistence that we eat them at the table.

Lucas picked *Atonement* even though it makes him cry because he has a crush on James McAvoy and I have crushes on

James McAvoy and Keira Knightley both, so it's all fair. Plus, period outfits? Pure bisexual chaos. Ezra fell asleep toward the middle and we paused the movie so Lucas could bring him back to bed.

I checked my phone and saw two texts (one from Zehra hoping I was having a great day and one from Xio asking about the English homework) and one missed call. My stomach did a backflip when I saw it was from Mom. As though my relationship with her hadn't soured enough before I found out what she'd done to Lucas.

I glanced back at the hall. Lucas and Ezra had disappeared, but I took my phone out back anyway. Mom picked up after four rings and said, "Where have you been all day?"

If she wanted to know where I was all the time, she shouldn't have shipped me across the country. "Busy," I said. The birds continued to twitter in the trees just beyond the backyard. The sun beat down overhead and it already felt like summer.

"Have you thought any more about coming home?"

I stepped out of the shade and hopped up on the railing, positioning my feet on either side so I wouldn't fall. Lucas hated it when I did that. "I've thought about it."

"And?"

Lucas and Ezra weren't visible through the window into their bedroom, but knowing they were there made me a little calmer. "I'm staying here."

Mom was quiet for so long I almost thought the call dropped. Then she said, "Are you angry with me?"

Lucas paces when he talks on the phone. I wondered if he paced this same porch talking to Mom this morning. "Kind of," I admitted. "You are the one who sent me away because you decided you couldn't handle being a parent anymore."

"That's not what happened."

"Lucas said he called you this morning," I said. "How'd that go?" I was suddenly furious. I might've blown up at her right then, but I resolved to ask Lucas if that was ok with him first before going off on his behalf. It was one of the hardest things I've ever had to do.

A beat. I toyed with my hair and waited. "I don't understand how that's relevant," she said.

"Actually, it is. I'd rather spend the summer with someone who stands up for me and understands who I am instead of someone who gaslights me and pretends like I'm crazy to her friends."

"I'm not going to stay on the phone with you if you're just going to be nasty."

"Ok. Bye." I hung up and set the phone face down in front of me. My hands shook a little bit and I took a deep breath. The screen door slid open and Lucas joined me on the porch. My heart pounded, but I tried to make my face casual. "How's Ezra?" I asked as Lucas came up next to me.

"Sleeping again," Lucas said. He glanced down at my phone and frowned. "Are you ok?"

I nodded. "I think so." It wasn't a lie. I *was* ok, or I was going to be. "Thank you for wanting me here."

Lucas blinked twice. "Of course," he said. "I love you, Avery."

I leapt down from the banister and gave him a quick hug. Another one. Jeez, we're becoming *those* people. "D'you want to finish the movie?" I asked. "You haven't even cried yet."

Lucas laughed. "Sure," he said. "It won't be long."

We went back into the house together and settled in our seats. I fiddled with the remote for a second. "Hey Lucas?" I said. "I'm not going back to California this summer." And maybe I'm too deep into AP lit, but I don't think I could describe Lucas's smile as anything but radiant.

After months of prep and eighty-five billion dresses, it finally happened! Last week was prom! I know it's totally cheesy for this to be the favorite part of my high school experience, but it's definitely up there. Connor's prom was the same day and Xio decided they didn't want a date just to say they had one, so all four of us went together, which is exactly how I wanted it. Lucas took the day off so he could bring me to get my hair and makeup done. The hairdresser straightened and then curled my hair, "So you'll have two styles once the curls relax," she said. I know nothing about hair, so I trusted her.

I finished and went back to Lucas, who stared at me. "You look like an adult," he said. There was an unmistakable waver in his voice.

I grinned. "I'm not even in my dress yet." Lucas and I have been doing really well recently. I think it has something to do with us being honest with each other. Surprise, surprise, that actually works. The night after he told me why he left California, we stayed up late talking and I told him what I'd told Ezra about my guilt around Devin and about how happy I am in my relationship with Zehra and more about how strange and empowering and sad and final it felt to reject Mom's offer to go back to California. I told him how I stayed up all night crying when he left for college and how I didn't have the energy to fight it by the time Mom and Dad sent me here and how much I love him. He listened the whole time and it was amazing just to talk about it all with him.

After, I asked him to tell me more about everything that happened with Mom and he did. He told me how alone he felt and how torn he was about me coming here and how much it hurt to see Mom treat me the same way she treated him. "You probably saved my life," he said at one point.

"What do you mean?" We'd moved to my room at that point and sat together against the pillows, passing a pack of Oreos back and forth.

"I don't know if you remember," he said. "I wasn't . . . I thought about trying again, after I got out of the hospital. Not immediately, but soon. You came to my room that night, climbed into bed with me, and demanded that I be ok. I couldn't bring myself to try again after that."

"I remember," I said softly. "Thank you for telling me." He offered me a small smile and passed the Oreos back. I took them and said, "I would have been devastated if anything happened to you."

"I know," Lucas said softly. "I know that now."

I think we're going to be ok. It's a weird feeling, but weird in a good way. I haven't felt like that in a really long time.

The first week after Lucas came out to Mom for the second

time, he was mostly worried about Ezra, even though Ezra was recovering fine. He slept on and off for the first three days and then he was pretty bored after that, since Lucas and his boss both insisted he take the week off work. Jess offered to go with Lucas to pick up Ezra's car, since Ezra wasn't supposed to drive for a bit, so they did that the Sunday after all the chaos.

Lucas flipped after they followed up with doctor and she told them not to watch any movies or anything, since that was the first thing we did after Ezra came home, but Ezra reassured Lucas he felt fine. He was frustrated more than anything about the meds and I don't blame him. He has to go back on the old stuff for a while since the new drugs made him so sick, but his doctor is working on getting him approved for another drug, so hopefully that goes better.

After Ezra went back to work, I think it hit Lucas that he actually, you know, came out to Mom. Neither of us heard from her all week and he finally had a total freak out Thursday night. The three of us were talking about my post-prom plans in the kitchen when Lucas stood up and straight bolted from the room.

Ezra and I exchanged wide-eyed glances before we followed Lucas into the living room. He was hyperventilating on the couch with his knees drawn up to his chest. His eyes bugged out of his head. Ezra sat next to him and slid his arms around Lucas' shoulders and Lucas buried his face in Ezra's shirt and burst into tears. "It's ok," Ezra whispered. "You're having a panic attack, but you're ok. I'm right here."

Lucas shook his head. "I can't breathe," he gasped. "I can't breathe."

"Yes, you can. You're ok." Lucas shook his head again and dissolved into sobs. I blinked back my own tears and Ezra held Lucas closer. "Shh, it's ok. You're safe, love. You're right here with me and Avery." He pressed a kiss into Lucas's hair. "Take a deep breath," he murmured. Another beat of strangled half-gasps and Ezra shook his head against the top of Lucas's hair. "Breathe, Lucas."

"I can't –"

"Yes, you can. With me." Ezra slowed his own breathing and after another beat, Lucas finally followed suit.

We sat there for a few minutes, just breathing, Lucas' breaths coming in easier but still hitching at the end. At last, he lifted his tearstained face. "I'm so sorry," he said. The sleeve of Ezra's shirt was damp.

"Don't be sorry," Ezra murmured. "What happened?"

Lucas held Ezra like they were caught in the ocean and Ezra was the one thing keeping him from drowning. "What if coming out to Mom was a mistake?" He looked at me, his eyes pleading, and I didn't know how to answer without making everything worse. "I'm sorry. I didn't mean for this to happen."

"Why was it a mistake?" Ezra asked, ignoring Lucas's second apology.

"I can't, I won't, I mean, I basically torpedoed any chance of having a relationship with her." He stumbled over his words and I almost started crying again.

"Lucas," Ezra said slowly, "you came out to her before and she was awful about it, but she didn't stop talking to you. She hasn't cut Avery off. She's homophobic and selfish but she's not going to ice you out, alright?" Lucas shook his head and buried his face back in Ezra's shirt and mumbled something. "What was that?" Ezra asked.

Lucas lifted his still-puffy face the fabric. "Why hasn't she called?"

"Because she never calls," Ezra said. He smoothed Lucas's hair back. "Lucas, sweetheart, nothing has changed. She's just like this." Lucas shuddered and Ezra held him close again. "Do you want to call her?"

"I don't know. I don't know."

"Ok." Ezra kissed his forehead, then his temple. "You don't have to decide right now. We're here for you."

I moved to the couch with the two of them and put a hand on Lucas' arm. "I don't think you made a mistake," I said quietly.

Lucas nodded and reached up to put his arm around me. I put my head on his shoulder and we just sat there for a little while longer like that, just quiet and breathing and together. Lucas did decide to call Mom the next day and he was a little calmer after he got off that call because Mom was less of a trash human than she could've been. Ezra says Lucas is probably going to go back and forth on how ok he is and we're just going to have to be there for him when it gets bad. I was never like that after I came out, but I'm accepting that Lucas and I are just different people and that's ok.

Anyway, I'm getting sidetracked. Lucas and Ezra took me to Xio's before the actual prom so we could all take pictures together. Zehra ran across Xio's backyard and kissed me quick. "You look amazing," she said. She traced a hand down the dark green fabric of my dress and I actually think I blushed.

"*You* look amazing," I said. Her dress was high-necked and white-ish gold. She carried matching sandals in her hand. Her makeup was the same pale gold and she looked like a freaking princess, ok? I don't know how I ended up with the most gorgeous girl on the entire East Coast, but I'm not complaining.

Xio and Owen caught up with us. "We all look amazing," Owen said. He wore a bright red suit with matching lipstick and Xio wore a black, strapless jumpsuit. "Now let's go take some photos so we remember how good we look when we're our parents' age."

We were there for a while and we took pictures together and with our families. All the parents loved Lucas and Ezra and it was fun to watch Lucas get shy in the face of all the attention. We all headed over to the high school after that for this thing they do in Millboro called "pre-prom," where all the seniors get together outside and all the parents and siblings and whoever can see all the dresses. Sometimes the younger grades come, so we saw a bunch of the kids from Pride. Ty told me he liked my hair, which was super sweet, and we talked to him and Shawn and Carmen for a while. Owen spotted Devin first, looking lost and bitter and very alone. Apparently, he'd just broken up with his third or fourth girlfriend of the year. I still have a lot of different feelings about what happened with Devin, but part of me is glad I have three amazing dates while Devin has no one. Is that petty? Maybe, but I get to be a little petty, I think.

After maybe half an hour I realized I didn't see Lucas and Ezra anywhere, so I texted them.

Me:
where are u guys?

Lucas:
Inside. We wanted to see your paintings!

I grinned to myself. All the art from Mrs. Chang's seniors was on display by the front desk. I told the others I was going to get Lucas and Ezra and followed them into the building. They were standing with their backs to me, in front of three of my paintings.

The first one was watercolor, so I wasn't as pleased with it as the other two. Acrylics are my thing, after all, but Mrs. Chang wanted me to try other things. It was pretty good for the medium. It was a portrait of Zehra from our portrait unit, where she's laughing at something I said as I snapped the reference photo. Her long hair is braided back and her eyes are crinkled at the corners. She's looking off to the side, but you can see the warmth in her gaze. There's paint on her blouse from class a few weeks before.

The second painting is one I did from memory, of Mom.

Toward the end of the class, Mrs. Chang said we could paint what we liked, so I went back to acrylics, of course. In the painting, Mom is looking down at a framed photo and leaning against the wall. She's tucking one strand of hair behind her ear, but it doesn't look like she's aware of her surroundings. I tried for "wistful," whatever that means, so her eyes are a little down-turned, her mouth curved down in a small frown. You can't see the photo, but I imagined it was me, or Lucas, or maybe both of us. The colors are pretty dark, browns and blues and greens. I didn't think about it much while I was painting it, but I guess my relationship with Mom is complicated. Not in the same way as her and Lucas' relationship, but still. I'm mad at her, but obviously she's still on my mind. I'm still figuring that out, too.

The last painting is an acrylic of Lucas and Ezra during a movie night. Ezra is leaning against Lucas and Lucas is looking down at him with so much love it hurts me a little to look at the picture. Lucas is wearing his favorite blue sweater and Ezra is in Lucas's Millboro sweater because that's *his* favorite thing to be in. They're holding hands across Ezra's chest. You can see the semicolon on Ezra's wrist.

I'd asked both of them if it was ok for Mrs. Chang to hang up the painting before she did it, since I'm not trying to out anyone. So they knew it was there, but I guess it was different seeing it in person. Lucas' head had fallen onto Ezra's shoulder and his arm was wrapped around Ezra's waist. I came up next to him and both of them looked at me. "These are amazing," Ezra said. "I knew you were the most talented person in the family, but wow."

I can't lie, I definitely flushed with pleasure at the compliment. "Thanks," I said. To Lucas, "What do you think?"

"I think," Lucas said slowly, "I couldn't be more proud of you than I am right now." He gave me a quick hug and I squeezed him so tight. Sometimes it hits me that in just a couple months I won't be living with him and Ezra anymore and I wish we had more time together. I'll have holidays and summer break in Virginia, but it won't be the same. Side effects of finally having a good relationship with my brother.

He pulled away and frowned. "What are you doing in here with us, though? The busses are about to leave!"

I rolled my eyes and we all came outside. I found my friends and Lucas and Ezra sent me off with a quick wave before we got on the busses to the prom venue. The actual prom place was a huge building the school rented that was probably used for things like weddings and Bat Mitzvahs. We ate these super fancy dinners while the DJ set up (fish for me and Xio and veggie for Zehra and Owen), then suddenly the opening notes of "HOT TO GO!" by Chappell Roan blasted through the speakers. "Will you dance with me?" Zehra asked, leaning forward.

I nodded and we excused ourselves. We went out to the middle of the floor and began slow dancing to a fast-paced pop song, but no one really looked our way. "I love you," she whispered.

I buried my face against her neck and grinned. "I love you, too," I said. I know, it's so cliché. Prom is such a cheesy time for a love confession, and I know we might not last, but I'm allowed a first love just like everybody else. Whatever happens next year, for now, I'm happy.

The song ended and Xio and Owen found us and the four of us all danced together. We basically coopted the middle of the dance floor the whole time, but no one seemed to mind. We danced like we were the only people in the room and did the robot and hugged each other after, like, every other song. Xio had a flask they'd managed to sneak in, but we didn't even break into it until after prom, when we went back to Owen's and all slept in sleeping bags on the floor together. My hair had uncurled at that point and was straighter than anything (thank you, hairdresser lady!) and none of us bothered to take off our makeup, but getting to be with these guys on our last big high school adventure?

I wouldn't have it any other way.

195

oday's the day! I feel like I've been dreaming about this moment all year and it's finally here! I do mean dreaming in the most literal sense. Like, I'd wake up from a dream where I was about to get my diploma only to realize it was mid-March and I had a midterm paper due the next day I hadn't started. Lots of anxiety. Would not recommend.

Anyway, an update. I sent an email to my old art teacher Mrs. Chang a few days ago letting her know I accepted a position at Providence Elementary and thanking her for being so supportive. She responded yesterday:

Hi Avery,

Of course I remember you! It's so great to hear from you, and congratulations on your graduation and your new job! You're going to be an amazing teacher. I've never taught elementary school, but if you need any art teacher tips in general or if you just want to catch up, please feel free to reach out.

All best,
Nina Chang

Speaking of old high school friends, it turns out Xio, Zehra, and Owen will also all be back in Millboro for the summer before Owen and I start work and Xio and Zehra go off to grad school. Zehra's girlfriend will be there for a few weeks in July, the one I met over the December break. I think Owen wants me to be bitter and annoyed about it with him, since he and his boyfriend are in another "off again" phase and Zehra and I are technically exes, but I like Cam and she makes Zehra happy. Plus, I'm happy being single right now and besides, Owen and Connor will get back together before the summer is over. They always do.

I'll miss Providence, but it'll be good to be home for a while. The plan is for Lucas to drive me back up in August and then I'll fly back down for his and Ezra's wedding in October. I'm supposed to get there a few days early for "best person/person-of-honor" duties and work was really cool about granting me days off before I even started, but I can't take all week, so Jess is stepping in to field all inevitable hysterical Lucas calls Monday through Wednesday. Though to his credit, he's mostly been good about the whole thing. I think he and Ezra have been together so long they basically feel married already. I'm excited about the wedding, but I keep teasing Lucas that it's because I'm planning to hook up with one of Ezra's hot Italian cousins. I was on FaceTime with them once and said that and Ezra quipped that he could totally make it happen, so now it's a running joke, much to Lucas's dismay. The only cousins Ezra actually has are the ones I've already met who are both partnered up and older than me, but Lucas seems to have forgotten that.

Lucas finally heard from Mom last week. This was after a month of begging her to RSVP so they can plan for the reception. Lucas says he's not mad about it, so I'm trying not to be either. The point is, Mom will be there come fall, so we'll have to put Jess on Mom duty once I take over Lucas duty. Mom is bringing Austin, at least, and all of us like him a lot, shockingly enough, so hopefully he'll be a little bit of a buffer. We've only met him over FaceTime calls, but he's super nice and I stalked his socials a few weeks ago, after they started getting serious. I found photos of him at Pride with his kids wearing one of those "Free Dad Hugs" T-shirts, so that gives me some hope.

Speaking of dads, I spoke to Dad earlier this week pre-grad. He was actually super supportive, happy for me, proud of me, blah, blah. For him, it was pretty emotional. I don't know if he's ever said the words "I'm proud of you" before, so progress. Not like Lucas, who says it every other breath. Mom and I talked last week and I was a little disappointed to find out neither of my parents would be here today – ok, fine, very disappointed – but like my therapist says, I have so many people who love me. Lucas and Ezra are probably sitting front and center already, at least an hour before most of the parents even get to campus. I bet Lucas even got a decent parking spot.

They got here last night and dumped their bags at their hotel before they came to pick me up. They both look really good, really happy. Ezra looks healthy for the first since he had to switch his meds again. He's gained some weight back and he doesn't have those dark circles under his eyes and he says the new stuff is actually working for his pain. We talk all the time over video, but it's different seeing him in person.

Of course, the first thing he did was show me new pics of Pia and Carlo because even after three years, neither of us can believe Lucas finally caved and let Ezra get cats. Lucas, who insisted for years that he didn't even really want a pet, and now his Instagram is about fifty percent Ezra, fifty percent pics of the babies. Even Jess's Insta is littered with photos of Pia and Frida playing together (Carlo is too shy).

"We're thinking about getting them another sibling," Ezra said with a wink when they came to my dorm.

"No," Lucas said, "*you're* thinking about getting them a sibling." He was smiling, though. Apparently, Ezra's been plotting to get another cat from a local rescue group for the last year or so and he's pretty sure Lucas is about to crack. He's probably right.

They offered to take my friends out to dinner with us, but most of my people were already with family, so it was just the three of us at my favorite Chinese place. We ordered our dishes (a rice bowl for me, lo mien for Lucas, and bao buns for Ezra) and as soon as the waiter left, Lucas cleared his throat.

"Before we eat, I just want to say how proud I am of you, Avery." Like I said, it's every other breath with him. He continued, "You've been through so much and not once did you let that stop you from accomplishing your dreams. I know this is just the beginning of an incredible journey for you and I'm so glad to get to be a small part of it."

His eyes shone with barely-suppressed tears and of course that made me start crying. I rolled my eyes and said, "Damn it, Lucas, you always do this."

Lucas laughed and stood. We hugged and broke away just in time to see Ezra wipe his eyes with his sleeve. I laughed, too. "Are you crying now?"

"The light in here is really bright," he protested. "And right in my eyes." Lucas leaned over and kissed Ezra on the cheek before

Ezra pulled him closer for a real kiss. The young family at the table next to us kept staring, probably trying to work out if this was a funeral or a celebration, but I didn't care.

Ezra insisted Lucas and I should get some time alone together, so we took a long walk around campus after dinner, just me and him. "I really am so proud of you," he said. "You're so talented."

"Well, I know that," I teased.

"You *are*," he insisted. When I refused to indulge him he asked, "Have you spoken to Mom recently?" We passed the entrance to the campus and circled back.

I nodded. "She told me I've become 'an incredible young person,' and then immediately said, 'Do you like how I said person and not woman?'"

Lucas laughed. "She's trying. When we talked about the wedding she actually acknowledged, you know, that she didn't know how to deal with me after my dad died."

"There was nothing to 'deal with,' Lucas. You're her son."

He shrugged. "We talked about what happened after I came out. The first time. She admitted she didn't handle that well." He still had a hard time saying "attempted suicide." Ezra told me a while ago that Lucas was working with his therapist on that.

I rolled my eyes. "Bare minimum." Surprise, it's not good practice to gaslight your kid so badly he nearly overdoses on prescription pills.

"She is trying," he said. "I want to give her a chance." We stopped along the water. Lucas nudged a rock with his shoe and we watched it tumble into the choppy waves.

"Will it be weird to have her at your wedding?" They'd seen each other a few times since Lucas' coming out, part two. We did the first holidays after that with Ezra's family in New York, but she did ask if Lucas and I would come out to California for a week over the summer, so we went just the two of us. Lucas and Mom had a long talk on that trip that I wasn't there for, but he told me about it after. She basically said she didn't understand, but she still loved him, which I think Lucas really needed to hear.

The holiday break after that, all three of us went back to L.A. and Mom didn't really know how to act around Ezra at first, but Ezra is the best, so of course she warmed up to him by day two. By the end, she even admitted she liked Lucas and Ezra together. I mean, who doesn't, but still. She came to Virginia for the holidays this past year and didn't even drink that much. She'd just started dating Austin so she wouldn't stop talking about that, of course, but it is nice that she's happy. It was her first time in Virginia, so I took her around and showed her where I did my senior year of high school. Xio came over at one point and Mom used they/them pronouns the whole time, which was a big deal for her. Again, bare minimum behavior, but I am happy she didn't deadname anyone.

"It might be a little strange," Lucas said. "I'm nervous."

"You won't even notice she's there," I said. "You and Ezra will be busy making heart eyes at each other the whole time."

He laughed again. "Probably." He turned to look at me. "I'm so excited to marry him."

"I know."

"I love him so much."

I rolled my eyes and grinned. "I know, Lucas. I lived with you for a whole year, remember?" He's gotten mushier somehow since they've gotten engaged, but I don't mind. They both deserve it and honestly, they're good for each other.

Lucas checked his watch. "C'mon, I'll drop you off and then Ezra and I should get going. It's getting late."

"It's not even ten!"

"I'm an old man, Avery."

"You're thirty," I muttered, but we did turn around. He put an arm around my shoulders and I slid my arm around his waist and we walked back together like that. It was incredibly awkward, trying to talk to each other like that, and after a while and my arm went a little numb. It was also very, very sweet getting to spend that time with him.

Most of all, it was us.

Acknowledgements

An incredible amount of people (and cats) believed in this story, and I'm so grateful for them all. Number one is Allison DeBusk, who encouraged and often fueled my out-of-pocket ideas when working on the fragmented pieces of what would later become this book. Thank you for always being available to offer insight and hypothesize about Lucas and Ezra's relationship and what clothes these characters might wear. You rock. Also Sammi Chiodi, who read bits and pieces of a half-formed idea when I was still scribbling scenes down in my notebook and encouraged me to keep writing Avery's story.

Thank you to Carson Risser, who decided that no, me waiting four months to read her thousand-word short story wasn't an unforgivable friendship offense and yes, she would be up for reading a significantly longer piece in a much shorter time span and offer invaluable feedback. To (the other) Allison Stalberg, who got rid of approximately half of Avery's filler words while also making me feel extremely validated about Ezra's story and how important it was to include a character with chronic pain. You're one of my favorite people and I love you lots.

Thanks to Michelle Malkin, who offered to read this story on the subway to and from work because she's the best. You had all of *Mexican Gothic* to read and you still made time for my rough draft. True friendship right there. You did read *The Southern Book Club's Guide To Slaying Vampires* first, but I still love you. Thank you to Beatriz and Elizabeth for being my Supportive Writing Friend and my Supportive Publishing Friend, respectively. I don't know what I would do without you both.

The start of this publishing journey was painful and chaotic, but I met some incredible people along the way. Thank you to Amanda, Elizabeth, Kenneth, Neal, Shauna, and Zoë for your love, support, and writer memes. It's been an honor and a privilege getting to know you and reading your books. Thank you to Eric, Laura, and Megan for all your advice. I wouldn't have been able to do this without you.

All I Know So Far is my first published young adult story, so thank you to Cass, Jenna, and Nina for recommending resources and offering their insight. Of course, thank you to Rachel for being there through the panic attacks, the imposter syndrome, and the general chaos that comes with writing a book. Best sibling ever. The Avery to my Lucas, but without the age gap or the inordinate amount of stress. Thank you to my furry baby, Artemis, for also being there, but with fewer braincells. You try your best.

Thank you to Lauren and Kota, who believed in my little story when I had a hard time doing it myself. Everyone at Inked

In Gray has been a delight to work with and I'm excited to do this all again, hopefully soon. Carlin (my cover artist) and Ginny (my editor) deserve a special shout out.

To my fantastic agent, Danielle D. Hunter, thank you for being there through all my chaos and self-doubt. It's been life changing to work with someone who's also queer and chronically ill and I'm so glad I met you. To Daffodil, my furry co-agent, for providing serotonin in the form of model shots via email.

Last but certainly not least, thank you to YOU, reading this right now. It means so much to me that you took a chance on Avery's story. I hope you liked spending time with her as much as I did.

The Dominique Nolan Center in Washington, DC, doesn't exist, but it is very heavily based on the Ali Forney Center, an LGBT Youth Shelter and Services in Manhattan, New York. Ali Forney was a gender nonconforming kid who was kicked out of their home at thirteen years old. Ali and their friends educated their community about HIV prevention and constantly advocated for further investigation into the murder of queer and trans youth. When Ali was murdered at age twenty-two, their friend Carl Siciliano founded the Ali Forney Center in Ali's memory. Check out the center's work at aliforneycenter.org.

The other places named during the Pride trip to DC are real places anyone can visit and Bayard Rustin was a real man who lived during and beyond the Civil Rights Era. The Bayard

Rustin Coalition is one such organization doing work in Bayard's name for queer and trans Black communities. Their website is bayardrustincoalition.com. The Trevor Project is also a real organization doing amazing work around mental health in the LGBTQIA+ community. Check them out at thetrevorpro ject.org.

Additionally, Ezra's work at a rape crisis center in the fictional city of Millboro is based on my time at the Orange County Rape Crisis Center in the very real city of Chapel Hill, North Carolina, with Briana Proctor and Kelly Taylor. You can see the incredible work they're doing at ocrcc.org.

All of the colleges named in the manuscript are real places, but heavily fictionalized, as I did not go to an art school myself.

In case it isn't clear, there is no right way to be LGBTQIA+, or struggle with mental health, or have a chronic condition. There is no right way to look queer or to chronically ill. The characters in *All I Know So Far* each have their own experiences, but so does everyone else. All experiences and identities are valid.

If you or a loved one are struggling with mental health, feel free to check out the following resources:

Active Minds: activeminds.org

Bring Change to Mind: bringchange2mind.org

National Suicide Prevention Lifeline: 988lifeline.org

The National Alliance on Mental Illness: nami.org/Home

Trans Lifeline: translifeline.org

The Trevor Project: thetrevorproject.org

About the Author

Nicole Zelniker (she/they) is the author of several books, including FROM WHERE WE ARE, which has been nominated for a Pushcart Prize. She's also the founder and editor-in-chief of the literary magazine Knee Brace Press. In her free time, Nicole enjoys re-reading her favorite books, listening to musicals, and bothering her cat.

If you enjoyed *All We Know So Far*, please consider also reading *Black Licorice*, or any of the other Inked in Gray novels and anthologies. Support our small business by buying direct at InkedinGray.com

We also appreciate any and all reviews! You may leave a review on Goodreads, Amazon, IndieStoryGeek or on our site at Inkedingray.com